**Mary Morgan
Tarzanne
Frida and Diego**

Seren Drama

GREG CULLEN

Mary Morgan
Tarzanne
Frida and Diego

seren

seren
is the book imprint of
Poetry Wales Press Ltd
Wyndham Street, Bridgend, Wales

ISBN 1-85411-223-6

A CIP record for this title is available from
the British Library

*The publisher works with the financial assistance of the
Arts Council of Wales*

Cover: Andy Dark

Printed in Palatino by The Cromwell Press, Trowbridge

Contents

Mary Morgan

Mary Morgan was originally commissioned by Theatr Powys for the inaugural production by the Mid Powys Youth Theatre in October 1987 at the Wyeside Arts Centre, Builth Wells. The production was co-directed by Guy Roderick and Greg Cullen. Musical Direction was by Steven Byrne and Janine Sharp. Choreography was by Rachel Freeman. The script won the "City Limits award for New Expressionism" in 1988 and was performed at the Riverside Studios, London, in a co-production with Red Shift Theatre Company and Mid Powys Youth Theatre, directed by Robert Rae. *Mary Morgan* was subsequently adapted for BBC Radio 4 and first broadcast in 1991, directed by Alison Hindell. This version of the script was first performed by students on the Performing Arts course at Coleg Powys, Newtown in 1994. That production was directed by Greg Cullen with Musical Direction by Steven Byrne.

Mary Morgan was originally written for Promenade performance, however the play can work just as well on a traditional stage. The stage directions relate to a Promenade production and are retained only to help the reader visualise the play. There were six stages used in the original production: A raised central stage in the round which is Wilkins's study; the courtyard of Wilkins's "castle", the Kitchen in Wilkins's house; the stable or hayloft which also served as Mary's bedroom and her prison cell (these three stages were down one side of the theatre); the shanty town and a river bank were opposite.

The King sits aloft a tall moveable tower. Within the tower, hidden until the courtroom scene, is Judge Hardinge's chair. The King's tower was moved to a new position for the

THREE PLAYS

courtroom scene during the arrival of Hardinge, the King's Judge, to Presteigne. A cart is used to take Mary around the auditorium/to the gallows.

The set and costumes should be an eclectic mix of periods and cultures, recognisable but unfamiliar.

The play is based upon a true story.

CHARACTERS

Servants
Mary Morgan
Molly Meredith
(Cook) Elizabeth Evelyn
Maggie Harvard
Gillian
John Kent

The Gentry
Walter Wilkins (Snr.)
Walter Wilkins (Jnr.)
George Hardinge MP

The Aristocracy
King George III
Catherine Devereux
The Earl of Hereford

Women of the Town
Hefina
Betty (Hefina's daughter)
Edwina
Sian
Kate
Bethan
Grace (a girl)
Sarah

A Militia Sergeant

Act One
SCENE ONE

WILKINS: The world changes.

WOMEN: (*chant builds*) Death to all Kings.

            (*The KING wakes suddenly from a nightmare. The women are drawn towards him.*)

WILKINS: Your Majesty?

KING: I saw the morning, in a dream.

WILKINS: Dream?

KING: A nightmare.

WILKINS: A nightmare?

KING: A vision.

WILKINS: Make your mind up.

KING: What? What did you say?

WILKINS: You saw the morning?

KING: Yes, yes. I saw the dead lie twisted in the sand smouldering within ruins. I saw neighbour massacre neighbour. I saw acid fall from the sky, watched a child, her skin on fire, running from her home.

WILKINS: Ah, you saw the war.

KING: Did I? We must go back. How did I allow it? Men

have risen from the soil to be proclaimed emperors. We have allowed clerks to lead armies, seen the company amass enough wealth to make Kings bow before them. When all is done they will come for me, salivating hounds, they gather in packs howling to be fed. The people blame me.

WILKINS: Don't feel too badly about it. The war is the only thing keeping you in power. Mind you, something's got to give sooner or later.

KING: Who are you?

WILKINS: An honest man.

KING: What is this place?

WILKINS: Your country.

SCENE TWO

(The shanty town. Women continue the action from where they finished the chant. They have been listening carefully to the KING and WILKINS.)

KATE: How can we pay for bread with the men at war?

BETTY: Hunger weighs like a stone, heavy in your belly.

SIAN: Evictions.

EDWINA: Taxes.

BETTY: Tolls.

HEFINA: Swollen-bellied children, pregnant with ghosts, riddled with phantoms chewing like worms through intestines.

EDWINA: When I belch these days I taste my own flesh rotting.

(SARAH approaches HEFINA. SARAH is disturbed but not without her wits.)

SARAH: Can you tell me where the war is today?

HEFINA: From here on, old woman, in any direction, even inside yourself.

SARAH: I had a dream last night which I must tell my children. Tell them to come home. It's lost now, y'know.

EDWINA: What is?

SARAH: The world, the King, I think. In this dream I awoke to find myself beside a womb. It was lying by a battlefield, shrivelled, twisted like salt beef, a silent contorted pain.

KATE: Perhaps it was yours. *(a joke)*

SARAH: I didn't know, how do you know what is yours anymore? The magpies pecked at it, not much of a meal in that, I can tell you. I'm sure my children went to war, I must tell them it's too late.

(The women assemble around the shanty town and make as if to begin the laundry.)

HEFINA: But the King lives, citizen, forget your children, love the King, the poor, mad King, bound by his feverish blankets, tangled in restless sheets woven by women's hands, women who also feed him.

BETTY: There now, good King, whom is heaven sent, suck me.

SIAN: Steal the milk from my baby, Cuckoo King.

EDWINA: The King is Cuckoo!

KATE: Oi! He's been sent us by God!

EDWINA: Then God is Cuckoo!

BETTY: We mop his brow whilst he steals our warmth.

KATE: Absorbs our heat whilst we shiver in his shadow.

BETHAN: We'll feed him our children, succulent and moist.

SARAH: In this dream as the womb decayed I could hear the voices of children suffering.

HEFINA: I hear them, old woman. We all do.

(GRACE appears through the crowd. The women stop and look at her. GRACE is an abused, violent and angry child. GRACE studies them, then chooses to speak to HEFINA.)

GRACE: I need a place.

BETHAN: Not another one. *(to GRACE)* This camp's full. You'll have to move on.

GRACE: You. *(to HEFINA)* I need a place.

HEFINA: Where's your mother?

(GRACE shrugs.)

HEFINA: Your father at war?

(GRACE nods.)

HEFINA: Brothers or sisters?

(GRACE shrugs.)

BETHAN: We're full.

BETTY: *(to HEFINA)* Mum, there's not enough work. She's probably got her whole family waiting round the river.

HEFINA: *(to GRACE)* Help me. Where's your family?

GRACE: Landlord put a man on the farm. Beat us. Made us do it. Mum ran off, took the little ones. Left me.

BETHAN: Yeah, I can see why an' all.

(GRACE pulls a knife on BETHAN.)

HEFINA: Stop! You can have what we have.

BETHAN: You're going to....

BETTY: Mum!

HEFINA: Cut willow for a shelter. Now put the knife away,
          it isn't doing anything. What's your name, dear?

GRACE: Grace.

SARAH: I can't tell where the war starts and ends. I'll ask
          the King. He'll know.

          (*WALTER enters on the SERGEANT'S shoulders, as
          if he is his horse. The SERGEANT wears a red military
          jacket. The women move rapidly to block his path.*)

WALTER: Move aside there, move aside!

EDWINA: Look at his horse, its coat like silver.

HEFINA: Gums like cherries, teeth like stone.

KATE: Mane like ribbons at a harvest fayre.

BETTY: His horse has a better life.

ALL: A better life.

WALTER: You women have no right to squat here.

HEFINA: And who might you be, young sir?

WALTER: I am Walter Wilkins, my father is Member of
          Parliament.

HEFINA: Well, that does make you important then.

BETTY: How would you like me to do your laundry?

HEFINA: Betty!

WALTER: This land has been designated a military camp.

BETHAN: Military?

HEFINA: Well, we ain't moving.

SARAH: Is he the King?

SIAN: No, Sarah, just thinks he is.

WALTER: Move aside!

BETTY: Give us the buttons off your coat.

KATE: His gut will, in time, grow fat and burst them anyhow.

BETTY: Give us the buttons to lay on our children's eyes.

KATE: Give us your gut to feed on.

EDWINA: That flesh belongs at my table, I'd know it anywhere, those cheeks were once my own.

HEFINA: That patch of soft flesh hanging beneath his chin like muslin full of fruit; it was my son's, I'm sure of it. I used to kiss it, suck it into my mouth and tickle it with my tongue tip to make him giggle. Why, I'm sure it was quite my favourite part of him! He lost it some months back, Master, tell me where did you find it?

WALTER: I don't know what you are talking about, woman. Now, out of my way before I call for your arrest. Lay not a hand upon me.

SARAH: Sir, I've lost where the war is, can you show me?

            (*WALTER strikes her down. The women retaliate. WALTER steers the SERGEANT/horse away from them and dismounts as he speaks. The actor playing the horse becomes the SERGEANT instantly.*)

WALTER: Sergeant!

SERGEANT: Yes, Sir?

            (*WALTER gives the SERGEANT instructions then oversees the scene.*)

GRACE: Them soldiers going to hurt us?

HEFINA: We'll see, Grace.

SERGEANT: Well, well, well, what's this? An illegal gathering? Master Walter's most upset.

14

HEFINA: No soldiers here! Get away from our camp!

SERGEANT: Now, now, now, that's no way to treat your new neighbours, is it?

BETTY: Get your hands off me!

SERGEANT: Careful now, the King might think you're threatening his peace!

SARAH: He knows the King?

SERGEANT: After all, us lads have been sent here to protect you, so don't hurt our feelings. You have no idea how my lads miss their women folk. Why the most curious things start happening to us. As each day passes it seems to get longer and harder until it's so long and hard, can't hardly concentrate on keeping the peace at all. Sad, in'it?

BETTY: You ought to lend each other a hand to get over it.

(*The women jeer and laugh.*)

SERGEANT: That's funny. See, I like that, life should have its pleasures and its rewards, shouldn't it? Otherwise, might as well jump in that river now. Pleasures and rewards, what d'you think?

SARAH: What's he talking about?

HEFINA: Keep your own company, and your blood money.

SERGEANT: Keep the money? I'm not sure you'd all agree with that, would you? I can pay you ten times what you earn now. None of us wants to be here, right? But at least this way we all benefit. What's your name, girl?

GRACE: Grace, sir.

SERGEANT: Grace. Tell your mother she should feed you properly.

GRACE: Never mind her, I'll let you do it to me.

HEFINA: Grace, shut up!

SERGEANT: Now I've heard everything. You call this living? When children talk like that?!

HEFINA: Now you get out!

BETHAN: He's right, money is bread.

HEFINA: Money is gin, you mean!

BETHAN: Gin is a better life.

SERGEANT: Now this woman understands me. How would you like to be my overseer?

BETHAN: Sure, I'd keep them in line. Bethan's the name.

(*The women object.*)

HEFINA: I'm in charge!

SERGEANT: In charge?

SARAH: Hefina saved us from the Parish.

SERGEANT: Well, she ain't going to save you from Master Walter, even if he is a jumped-up little pillock!

(*Some women laugh.*)

WALTER: Everything in order down there, Sergeant?

SERGEANT: Yes, sir, no problem. (*to women*) No, I think she's gathered you here to fill your minds with foreign ideas.

BETHAN: That's right! She has. I've heard her say how we should do what the French did to their King.

SERGEANT: A witness! Right, anyone who fails to swear allegiance to me, the King's representative, get out! What's it to be, the King or the Poor Law?

HEFINA: No-one wants your company.

BETTY: Mum, don't. We're hungry and each week it gets worse.

HEFINA: (*shocked*) It'd be your flesh on the plate.

BETTY: No, just bacon, potatoes, bread.

BETHAN: Ha! Listen to her daughter!

HEFINA: Did I bring you up to become pig's meat? (*pause*) I'd kill you before I saw that happen.

BETTY: Oh well, kill me. I'd hate to see you lose your self-respect.

(Suddenly, HEFINA attacks BETTY with a scream. Panic amongst the others. The SERGEANT thumps HEFINA.)

WALTER: Sergeant!

SERGEANT: Sir! She's just leaving.

WALTER: Good.

BETTY: No, let her stay. She's learned her lesson.

WALTER: Any more objectors and they go too, Sergeant.

SARAH: Well, your Majesty, I'm going if Hefina's going!

SERGEANT: Good luck, dear!

SARAH: Come on, Betty, help her up.

BETTY: No, I'm staying.

SARAH: What?

SERGEANT: Are you the overseer or not?

BETHAN: Yes. Yes, sir. Get back into the camp! All of you. Come on, I said move.

SARAH: Betty? Come back.

WALTER: You've settled yourself in very quickly, Sergeant.

BETHAN: Move!

SERGEANT: Delegation, sir.

(The SERGEANT exits with WALTER on his shoulders. SARAH helps HEFINA away. BETHAN harangues the women back into the camp. BETTY looks back at her mother.)

17

SCENE THREE

KING: By what right do you raise armies on my soil?

WILKINS: The right which says that my home is my castle. I shall protect it, and of course, you, your Majesty.

KING: Now I see you! A little Bonaparte.

WILKINS: You send your lads to fight against revolutions to ensure that no revolution breaks out here. The war impoverishes and displaces the populace and so in turn they renew their reasons for revolution. Ultimately, I'd say you were in a bit of a bind.

KING: I forbid private militias.

WILKINS: Of course. Meanwhile, if you should ever have need to re-establish order in your Kingdom, do not hesitate to call upon my services.

KING: Our head shall not roll so easily as a French head. Our head is quite firmly attached. I've been exercising the muscles of late and shall continue to do so. It shall never be entrusted to those who would discard the head in favour of a hat that glitters. Move against me and you move against God! You shall find yourself in hell. Hell! Where one can hear one's own thoughts rebound like swords against the helmet.

(*The King declines into his madness.*)

WILKINS: (*Smugly*) God's wisdom knows no bounds, as you shall discover.

SCENE FOUR

(*MARY, MOLLY and GILLIAN take down sheets and fold them into baskets in the courtyard.*)

GILLIAN: She looks like a turkey with her head up high.

MARY: I never saw such a woman. How she ties that bow on her backside, what does she think? I hope her husband helps her with it, must take her hours otherwise.

MOLLY: Her husband! He's as useful as the hair on his chest.

GILLIAN: They argue like two rats over bacon rinds.

MOLLY: When I get made up to under-cook I won't have to take her orders no more.

COOK: (enters) Molly? Mary Morgan, what are you doing out here?

MOLLY: Mrs Harvard told me and Mary to help get these sheets in before it rains.

COOK: Did she now? Well, you're kitchen maids and you're my staff so don't you go taking no orders from her again. Where is she?

MOLLY: Went into the house. (imitates MAGGIE)

COOK: Don't cheek her in my hearing, wouldn't be fair if she was to hear.

MARY: I tell you what Maggie Harvard reminds me of.

MOLLY: What's that?

COOK: I'm not listening to any of this.

MARY: An old nag my father once took in. He'd a reputation for rejuvenating knackered horses see, only this one was past it, so just before the owner arrived to collect it he rolled a ball of pepper and stuck it up its arse.

MOLLY: Oooh, God!

MARY: Aye, perked it up no end, I can tell you. That's Maggie Harvard for you, an old nag with pepper up her arse.

COOK: Shush! She comes.

(MAGGIE HARVARD enters like a horse with pepper up its arse. She is justly paranoid and defensive. She wears an outrageous bow tied on her backside.)

MAGGIE: Cook.

COOK: Maggie. I'd be pleased if you consulted me before taking my staff.

MAGGIE: I had already waited an abnormal amount of time for your appearance, so considered myself justified. I presume they may continue?

COOK: Maggie, a word. Now you speak to me like that again and I will have no option but to humiliate you. And considering the complications of your other relations to this house, that would not be difficult. Stay where you are! You wait for as long as I take. I'll not have these girls getting above themselves for the want of a better example from you.

MAGGIE: Have you finished?

COOK: We're too long in the tooth to still be at war, Maggie. Time you settled down, isn't it?

GILLIAN: What do we do now? I think it might rain.

MOLLY: Here it comes.

MAGGIE: Quickly, get them in.

(WALTER arrives on his horse [JOHN KENT] and dismounts.)

WALTER: Best get a move on, Cook.

COOK: Aye, Master Walter.

WALTER: John. *(The rain starts. John now mimes holding a horse's reins as if he were a stable lad, which he is.)*

WALTER: Come on, Mrs Harvard!

(WALTER playfully lends a hand.)

MAGGIE: It's quite all right, Master Walter.

(The rain worsens. Everybody is getting soaked. WALTER whips up the hilarity of their panic. WALTER notices MARY.)

WALTER: Come on, young lady.

(They are all laughing except MAGGIE. WALTER goes too far and throws a sheet onto the ground. The women stop and look at it; wasted labour.)

MAGGIE: That's not funny, Master Walter, you do go too far.

WALTER: Well, I... are you telling me off, Mrs Harvard?

COOK: I'm sure she wouldn't dream of it, Master Walter, and if she were insolent I or the housekeeper would deal with it. Now, bring those sheets into the kitchen. Mary, bring in the rest. *(MARY is left behind.)*

WALTER: Have I caused you much work?

MARY: It will be all right.

WALTER: What's your name?

MARY: Mary Morgan, sir.

WALTER: Did I make you laugh?

MARY: You did, sir.

WALTER: It is hard work?

MARY: Sir?

WALTER: When do you relax? *(no reply)* Have you seen the river yet?

MARY: Many's the time, sir.

WALTER: Oh. You should go there on Sunday.

MARY: Oh no, sir.

21

WALTER: Why not?

MARY: I work this Sunday, sir.

WALTER: When shall you get a chance?

MARY: To see the river again, sir?

WALTER: Yes.

MARY: When I go into town, sir, for the market. I see it then.

WALTER: Good.

MARY: But I can't say I find it all that relaxing.

WALTER: No.

MARY: Perhaps I've not seen the right parts of it, sir. (*She holds out a sheet for him to help her fold.*)

WALTER: Why yes, that must be it. I shall go to the river Sunday week I think. Taking the footpath down for a mile or so, there is a stretch of river so beautiful you can quite forget who you are. You should visit it after lunch. (*They finish folding a sheet at this precise moment.*)

WALTER: (*to JOHN*) Why stand there, man? Get the horse inside! Fool. Good day, Mary Morgan.

          (*WALTER goes*)

JOHN: I don't like him messing with you like that!

MARY: Don't get jealous, John. He was only playing.

          (*MARY exits*)

JOHN: Yeah, well (*to horse*) I don't like it, do I, boy? Come on, hup! (*leads horse away*)

          (*MARY crosses to the kitchen stage where the other women are waiting to see what has happened between her and WALTER. They move away from imaginary windows and resume an occupied state. MARY enters. No-one makes eye contact with her.*)

SCENE FIVE

WILKINS: Walter? (*WALTER freezes*) Walter, is that you? (*Pause before WALTER tries to gently and silently continue on his way.*) Walter! Now, I know it's you. Come in here. (*WALTER gives up and enters the study.*) You're drenched!

WALTER: Yes, father.

WILKINS: Get off the carpet, you're making it wet! Look what you've done. This came from a Prince's palace in Chittagong, look at it!

WALTER: Perhaps, then, I can go and change my clothes after all?

WILKINS: No, I want to hear the news.

WALTER: The Militia's arrival came as a complete surprise.

WILKINS: Good. And the squatters...?

WALTER: They were unable to muster much resistance. I don't see why we don't just clear them off the land now.

WILKINS: I don't want them running around causing chaos all over the country. I want them controllable, in one place.

WALTER: I see.

WILKINS: Perhaps I should accept the Company's offer to send you to India. One has the chance to discover these things for oneself there.

WALTER: Then let me go.

WILKINS: Perhaps, if things get worse.

WALTER: I am bored with the Bank and the Estate. I am a book keeper!

WILKINS: I need you here. Besides, I want you safe.

WALTER: But there's nothing to do. You're off enjoying yourself in Parliament half the year. All I get is local balls with ruddy-faced Radnorshire heifers stomping on my feet. We are not deemed fit an invite to any finer society, what am I to do?

WILKINS: (*appreciating his son's humour*) Put your faith in the impatience of war. The old families, even the King himself, is coming to realise that we are indispensable. You shall have a wonderful life, Walter. Now, go and dry yourself. We don't want you catching a chill. What are you?

WALTER: Your only boy.

WILKINS: My only boy. (*he kisses WALTER*) Now go.

SCENE SIX

KING: I wonder what time it is?

WILKINS: It is still the middle of the night, your Majesty.

KING: I don't trust the morning. I can tell, I have seen it. I'm not allowing tomorrow.

WILKINS: No, your Majesty?

KING: We'll go back to yesterday.

WILKINS: But, your Highness, it took us all day yesterday to get here. Besides, what was so great about yesterday?

KING: I had mongrels like you at my heel and shall again. I have a little plan.

WILKINS: Oh, really? (*casually*)

KING: Yes. Bet you can't guess what it is?

WILKINS:	(*bored*) You're right, I can't. (*pause*) Well?
KING:	Well, what?
WILKINS:	Well, what is it?
KING:	Not telling. Not yet. From here I can see everything. You forget that.
WILKINS:	Down here I can feel what's going on. Don't you underestimate that!

SCENE SEVEN

(*MARY and MOLLY, looking their best, take an afternoon stroll down by the river. They talk as they walk to the river bank.*)

MOLLY:	The truth of it is only guessed at mind, you know how these are, no-one will tell you anything.
MARY:	I can't see her ever doing it! I can't imagine her.
MOLLY:	I can't imagine him.
MARY:	What a picture!
MOLLY:	They say that Wilkins paid George Harvard ten pound to marry Maggie.
MARY:	Ten pound!
MOLLY:	Aye and he's still drinking his way through it.
MARY:	Poor Maggie.
MOLLY:	Not so poor, at least Wilkins kept her on, not many men want their bastard child growing up around them. She's had it lucky. How much further?
MARY:	Oh, I don't know. I wasn't going anywhere particular. Bit further?

MOLLY: I'm hungry.

MARY: When you're under-cook, you'll have keys. You can bring us up cakes and meats to eat in bed.

MOLLY: Oh, I don't know about that, Mary. More than my job's worth. I think you'll have to be satisfied watching me eat.

WALTER: Hello.

MOLLY: Sorry, Master Walter, we had no idea you was....

WALTER: That's all right, Molly. I was just thinking that I'd like some company.

MOLLY: Well, sir, we've to be going I'm afraid.

WALTER: (*to MARY*) Is that so?

MARY: Well....

WALTER: I've got a picnic with me that I cannot eat alone. Please help me not to waste it.

MOLLY: Oh well, I suppose that would be wrong.

WALTER: Please sit. (*WALTER only has two of everything.*) Here, some wine. (*He gets a glass and pours some.*) Ah, wait, I'll rinse my glass in the river.

MARY: Don't worry, we'll share.

WALTER: Yes?

MOLLY: Yes.

WALTER: Well now, a cake? (*They each take one and eat.*)

MOLLY: We were just talking about cake.

WALTER: Really?

MOLLY: You haven't got one.

WALTER: Oh, that's fine, fine, don't worry. Well, cheers. (*They chink glasses, the women are having a wonderful treat. Long pause.*) Do you want an apple?

MOLLY: After you, sir.

WALTER: Well, all right. (*He takes one. Mary takes the other. Molly is left watching them. She realises that WALTER must have been expecting a guest and that it was MARY.*)

MARY: Here, we can share it.

WALTER: Here, my knife. (*He hands her his knife.*) Oh, let me do it for you. (*He takes back the apple and knife and makes a job of cutting it. MARY finds his courtesy and innocence of her ability to use knives amusing. MOLLY smiles back at her. MARY is engaged by WALTER.*) There!

MARY: Thank you, sir.

          (*WALTER watches her eat, forgetting that he has not given any to MOLLY who then has to lean with an effort across the picnic to pick some up.*)

WALTER: I am sorry.

          (*There follows a sequence of looks. WALTER looks at MARY. She catches his eye. They look to see if MOLLY has seen them. MOLLY looks down. Silence persists.*)

MOLLY: Lovely part of the river.

MARY: Yes, it's my favourite part. You can quite forget who you are.

MOLLY: You what? (*She gets up to look at the river.*) I think I'll just go over there. (*She gives MARY a stern look of warning behind WALTER'S back. MARY indicates for MOLLY not to leave her. WALTER looks up. MARY smiles at him. MOLLY walks away, indicating to MARY that she won't go far. It becomes mixed with amusement.*)

WALTER: I'd given you up.

MARY: Sir? (*she teases him*)

WALTER: I was wrong to, wasn't I?

MARY: To have what, sir?

WALTER: To have given you up?

MARY: Lovely afternoon for a walk, sir. (*she smiles*)

WALTER: Why don't we meet again?

(*Lights fade.*)

SCENE EIGHT

(*WILKINS sits. MAGGIE stands waiting to ascend the stage. They look at each other for some time.*)

WILKINS: Come in. (*MAGGIE enters holding WILKINS'S gaze.*) Have you seen Judge Hardinge? He went in search of more Cognac. He's pissed, so be warned.

MAGGIE: You want me to find him?

WILKINS: No. Come here. (*He pulls her astride his lap.*) Now, what's the matter? (*MAGGIE shrugs, WILKINS sighs*) How's that husband of yours? (*MAGGIE does not wish to hear mention of him.*) How have you been? (*MAGGIE feels sorry for herself.*) Poor Maggie. (*He cuddles her like a sad child. She kisses him.*) And how is the boy?

MAGGIE: You should see him. He's getting big and strong, handsome too.

WILKINS: Does he need anything?

MAGGIE: Schooling, sir, please send him to school. He's that bright, sir, you'd be proud of him.

WILKINS: I'll see. In future, when I send for you, obey me.

MAGGIE: It is not always possible, sir.

WILKINS: Make it possible.

MAGGIE: If I were housekeeper I wouldn't have to make excuses.

WILKINS: Don't be ambitious, Maggie. It makes me think you have no feelings for me. (*He starts to unbutton her blouse.*)

MAGGIE: If you're concerned about ambitions watch for Mary Morgan.

WILKINS: Which one is she?

MAGGIE: Kitchen maid. Pretty. The one cook wants to make under-cook.

WILKINS: Do you think I'd like her? (*MAGGIE gets up.*)

MAGGIE: No, sir, she's just a peasant girl. She's nothing to offer in the way of manners nor I would say, discretion, which is why I'm so concerned.

WILKINS: What is she saying?

MAGGIE: Nothing, but her actions are obvious. She's carrying on with Master Walter. Has been these past two months.

WILKINS: (*He is momentarily pleased and surprised.*) But she lacks discretion?

MAGGIE: She's quite proud of herself, sir. She's ambitious too.

WILKINS: Oh dear.

MAGGIE: What's more, Master Walter seems recklessly in love with her and is behaving in much the same fasion.

WILKINS: He would be. What should I do? (*He attempts to assess her motives.*)

MAGGIE: Get rid of her.

WILKINS: No, it'll do Walter good, be good experience. It will soon pass. Falling in love with one's servants is a, perhaps despicable, but necessary phase in a young man's life. But listen and be my eyes. If she becomes boisterous or worse I expect to be told. I can see all around me but that which is under my very feet. (*She touches him.*) Perhaps I may have cause to be rid of her. Anyway, wouldn't I be a terrible hypocrite if I did?

(*HARDINGE enters.*)

HARDINGE: Wilkins! Cognac! Who said I couldn't find the cellars? Oh! Excuse me.

WILKINS: Maggie, you've met my cousin, Judge Hardinge.

MAGGIE: Yes, sir.

HARDINGE: My dear Mrs Harvard. (*to WILKINS*) Well, I was going to admonish you for keeping a slovenly staff, Wilkins, but on second thoughts, perhaps I'll join you.

WILKINS: Maggie is special, Hardinge.

HARDINGE: Ah, yes. Well, get me another. I'm certainly not going to stand here and watch you.

WILKINS: You've to be in Brecon tomorrow to begin your circuit.

HARDINGE: I'll be there or make my own excuses!

WILKINS: How can you bear to preside over these courts; sheep rustlers, petty thieves, prostitutes?

HARDINGE: Well, you tell me how a man of talent is supposed to progress in this country, Wilkins?

WILKINS: You should encourage the Company to sponsor you in Parliament. I could arrange it for you.

HARDINGE: The Company? They are done for, old boy.

WILKINS: What d'you mean?

HARDINGE: There's a Bill, rumour is the King's behind it, they want to dismantle the Company, slice it up. It's grown too big, it rivals the power of the British

State, old boy, profoundly undemocratic proposition.

WILKINS: (*to MAGGIE*) Get off me! Damn the King!

HARDINGE:Now, now. There's nothing to be done, old chap. The old families will vote with the King. They will have a majority as always.

WILKINS: And you wonder why men of talent like you are left to preside over the theft of a pig or a bag of grain? You call that democratic, do you?

SCENE NINE

(*MOLLY and MARY are in their bedroom. MOLLY is fed up with MARY. HARDINGE and WILKINS are still visible in his study. They drink.*)

MOLLY: My face cloth is damp.

MARY: I only wiped my face on it.

MOLLY: I told you to leave my things alone!

MARY: Sorry, mine was....

MOLLY: Since you've come here I've nothing left.

MARY: Look, I'm sorry. I've done nothing against you.

MOLLY: Put your shoes away! Why must I always be falling over your shoes.

(*MARY puts her shoes away and gets into bed. A long, tense silence follows.*)

MARY: Maybe I should ask to share another room?

MOLLY: I don't know that anyone would want to share with you.

MARY: This hasn't got anything to do with untidiness

31

and you know it.

MOLLY: Don't tell me what I'm angry about! I'll decide that much. That much at least is mine to decide!

MARY: Molly....

MOLLY: And you keep out of it. (*pause*) I think you should move. I think the under-cook deserves better than this, don't you? Poor you, having to share with a lowly kitchen maid.

MARY: That's what this is about. I never asked for the job.

MOLLY: No, but you got it. Six years I've been here! It was my job.

MARY: Have it! I'll say I don't want it! Have it! Anything is better than this.

(*HARDINGE and WILKINS laugh, leaving the study they walk through the audience towards the maids' bedroom.*)

MARY: That's the master. Why's he coming up here?

MOLLY: He's got Judge Hardinge staying, have you seen him?

MARY: No.

MOLLY: All the young society ladies admire him. He's supposed to be most amusing.

MARY: They're coming up here.

MOLLY: Must be drunk.

(*The men enter the bedroom.*)

WILKINS: Good evening, ladies. We hope we're not disturbing you.

MOLLY: No, sir.

WILKINS: This, good ladies, is Judge Hardinge. Never mind who he is except to say he is both family and friend. Allow me to introduce... what's your name, my dear?

MOLLY: Molly, sir.

WILKINS: Molly. Ah (*Upon seeing MARY, he whispers into HARDINGE'S ear that MARY is WALTER'S.*)

HARDINGE: Indeed. Well, I won't intrude where I'm not needed. (*they laugh*) Wilkins, your Molly is a dove! May she truly fly into my humble nest?

WILKINS: A dove sharing a nest with an old buzzard?

HARDINGE: I might take offence at that.

MOLLY: If you please, sir, I'd rather be left alone.

WILKINS: Don't be impertinent, girl!

HARDINGE: Now, now, Wilkins, don't shout. There's no need. Come child. I won't hurt you. Here, there now.

(*MOLLY goes with HARDINGE. She glares at MARY. WILKINS looks at MARY, strokes her hair.*)

WILKINS: As for you, Mary Morgan. I think we'd best leave you alone. Learn discretion, my girl, and you'll be cared for.

(*WILKINS kisses her then leaves the stage to cross back to the study. The KING chuckles.*)

SCENE TEN

KING: Got you! I have calculated our support in both Houses for this bill. We shall not fail. We shall control our own destiny, Wilkins. Our crown will never fall into your basket. If you dare to move against me now, with a war on, no-one will support you. The Company's sun is setting in the west, Wilkins.

SCENE ELEVEN

(*The kitchen. Soup is being served to COOK, GILLIAN, MOLLY, MOLLY and JOHN by MARY.*)

COOK: All right, Mary, serve the supper.

MARY: Put the bowls out, Molly.

MOLLY: Please. You say please to me. No-one asks for nothing anymore.

MARY: Please could you put the bowls out, this soup is burning my hands.

(*MOLLY slams the bowls down.*)

JOHN: Soup? I like something solid for supper.

MARY: Then eat the bowl, John, eat the bowl.

GILLIAN: This is lovely soup, Mary. Did you make it?

MOLLY: Oh, shut up, Gillian.

COOK: Will you stop squabbling and eat? This has been going on for months and I've had enough of it.

(*MARY grabs her shawl and makes to leave.*)

MOLLY: Going out again, are we?

MARY: Want some air, that's all.

JOHN: This is a fine business.

COOK: John, eat your soup.

MARY: It's good soup, I made it special for you all.

(*pause*)

COOK: Very nice, Mary.

GILLIAN: Yes, Mary, very nice.

(*MOLLY and JOHN looks daggers at GILLIAN.*)

GILLIAN: I was just saying!

(MARY exits the kitchen pursued by COOK. MAGGIE enters the kitchen and observes them as if through a window.)

COOK: Mary, a word. *(pause)* You make life difficult for yourself, Mary. You been under-cook three months and you still haven't learnt.

MARY: Make Molly under-cook, I've had enough.

COOK: You can't be friends with them, Mary. If you want to be in charge of this kitchen then start learning to keep a distance between yourself and those below you. It makes difficult decisions easier. That's life. I hope you don't find that out the hard way.

MARY: No, Cook. I'll remember it next time you do me a favour.

(MARY walks away. We follow COOK back into the kitchen.)

MAGGIE: I was just asking after Mary. My, you are a sullen lot. Well, have you seen your friend, John?

JOHN: Yes, we've seen her.

MAGGIE: How is she? *(pause)* Shame about you two, isn't it?

GILLIAN: Mary's gone to get some air.

MAGGIE: My, did you ever know a girl in need of so much air as Mary Morgan?

COOK: Maggie, you wanted something?

MAGGIE: Just wondered if you'd heard the news, like?

COOK: What news? Well?

MAGGIE: The Earl of Hereford is coming to visit.

COOK: An Earl?

MAGGIE: That's not all. He's bringing his daughter Catherine with him. Now why would that be?

Judging by the way the master's behaving I think he's expecting great things for Master Walter.

SCENE TWELVE

(*MARY has gone to the stables where WALTER waits for her.*)

MARY: Can I come play in your hayloft, Mister?

WALTER: Only if you promise to be good. (*MARY climbs into the hayloft.*) I do love you, Mary.

MARY: Ssh.

WALTER: I do. I do. What's the matter?

MARY: Nothing. You're all I got left, Walter. You better love me.

WALTER: Now, what's wrong?

MARY: No-one talks to me no more.

WALTER: They are jealous. You are brighter than they are. You must learn to rise above them. Besides, with luck we'll both be gone before the year is over.

MARY: How?

WALTER: I have some money! There are new countries, Mary, with new rules. We can be together.

MARY: New rules?

WALTER: Yes. I've written something for you. Here. No, don't read it now, I'll be too embarrassed.

(*He hands her a letter. WILKINS shouts across.*)

WILKINS: Walter? Are you over there?

WALTER: God, it's my father!

MARY: Stay quiet.

WALTER: No, he'll come and look. (*to WILKINS*) Yes, father?

WILKINS: I've got some great news.

WALTER: (*to WILKINS*) Just checking Zephyr's hoof. Hmm, all seems fine! (*MARY laughs at him.*) (*to MARY:*) Something's cheering him up. I'll get rid of him and come straight back. (*to WILKINS*) Coming!

SCENE THIRTEEN

(*Kitchen. Great jollity amongst the staff.*)

COOK: We'll have salmon and pheasant and ooh! Me, cooking for an Earl!

(*They laugh.*)

MOLLY: Maybe we'll all get new clothes.

JOHN: Aye, there'll be a lot of changes hereabout.

MAGGIE: It's nice to see you smiling again, John.

JOHN: Well, Mrs Havard, it's about time we were all put back in our rightful places, in'it?

MOLLY: Here, here.

JOHN: Some of us need reminding.

COOK: Now, now, John, don't spoil it. Eat your soup.

JOHN: I don't want no soup!

GILLIAN: I'll have it.

COOK: John!

JOHN: Keep it. It's time I went for a breath of fresh air an' all.

COOK: John Kent, you stay here.

JOHN: The air belongs to everyone, Cook. And I'm going to take my share!

SCENE FOURTEEN

(*The hayloft. MARY reads the letter from WALTER. Her reading is unsure but she can work it out.*)

MARY: My darling Mary,
There is a clear day coming.
When I can see for miles.

(*JOHN KENT has gone to the stables. He makes a noise which MARY hears.*)

MARY: Walter? (*She waits. JOHN stays still.*) No use you trying to creep up on me. I heard you. (*She waits.*) I'll read your poem out! (*She waits.*) Right then, prepare to die of embarrassment. (*She reads.*)

On that clear day all I shall see is you
And between us a simple track to follow
There and then we shall truly meet.

(*A slight pause.*)

Don't be embarrassed. It's lovely.

(*JOHN climbs the ladder. MARY jumps.*)

JOHN: Yes, real sweet in'it, Mary?

MARY: What do you want?

JOHN: You're a working girl, you shouldn't be reading. Who's it from? Give it me!

(*They tussle over it.*)

MARY: Leave it alone! You'll be in trouble.

JOHN: Who with?

MARY: Let go!

JOHN: Who with? Who's going to make trouble for me?

MARY: The Wilkins!

JOHN: You mean Master Walter? Well, he ain't coming back. Not when he hears what his father has to say. So now who's going to make trouble, eh?

MARY: He'll whip you!

JOHN: He's gone to bed, girl, said I should take his place as a favour, like.

MARY: Give me the letter, it's mine, to me!

JOHN: What's the matter, Mary, you only go with the Master's boy, is that it? What's the matter with your own kind? Look, I just want it to be like it was. You used to like me touching you. Please, Mary. I'll marry you even. I want to. What'll you get from him? Need more than love letters to feed a child on.

MARY: Get off! Now give me the letter.

JOHN: And if I don't?

MARY: I'll tell him.

JOHN: No, you won't, girl, you won't say nothing about what happens here tonight. I'll tell you why. One word from you and this letter goes straight to Mr Wilkins. What'll he say about it, I wonder? Specially with Lady Catherine coming to stay, like.

MARY: Who?

JOHN: Earl of Hereford's daughter. Old Wilkins is going to marry her off to Walter. You'll be out of job my girl. Starve, you will.

MARY: Touch me and I'll kill you.

JOHN: You was going to give it anyway. Let him stick to

'is own kind. You're one of us, Mary Morgan. I'm
only taking what's mine.

MARY: No!

SCENE FIFTEEN

(Lights up on KING.)

KING: I'm cold. I'm cold.

WILKINS: What about jumping up and down, my Lord?

KING: Why have I been left to grow cold?

WILKINS: His Majesty feels neglected. Let us warm him.

*(The shanty town women rush amongst the audience
saying the verse. They finally threaten the KING. Then
they turn on WILKINS who clicks his fingers to herald
the entrance, at the end of the verse, of BETHAN.)*

WOMEN: Words and whispers
Pass the word around
Uprising, uprising,
The dead rise from the ground
Tonight in anger
We burn the masters down.

BETTY: What have we to fear that we aren't already
cowed under by?

BETHAN: What's going on? No gatherings! You've been
warned. I see you, Grace. And you, Betty. *(The
women stop.)* Get back to your homes before I call
the Sergeant to you!

*(The women disperse back to the shanty town. Lights
change to daylight.)*

SCENE SIXTEEN

(MARY enters with the COOK. Daylight.)

COOK: Are you unwell?

MARY: I feel better now.

COOK: Look at these females. They're a disgrace. None of them are from the town, you know. All come in from the country. Ought not to be allowed here.

BETTY: Mary Morgan!

COOK: Do you know her?

MARY: Betty.

(The meeting becomes awkward as BETTY remembers what she has become in comparison to MARY.)

BETTY: You look good. You still in service then?

MARY: I'm under-cook now, come to buy vegetables. This is Elizabeth Evelyn, the Cook.

BETTY: Pleased to meet you. *(COOK ignores her.)* Well, I won't keep you.

MARY: How are your parents?

BETTY: Father died. Mother got sent out of the camp. I thought perhaps you'd heard word of her.

MARY: Sorry, I never hear any news. Don't you and George have the farm then?

BETTY: George is at the war.

MARY: You must be very proud.

(BETTY is surprised by MARY'S naivete.)

BETTY: Service. Your's is a better life.

(A soldier calls.)

SOLDIER: Hey, Betty, how long are you going to keep me waiting?

	(*Pause.*)
BETTY:	(*to MARY*) Go away.
SOLDIER:	I said how long....
BETTY:	I heard you!
BETHAN:	Betty, you've got a customer waiting!
BETTY:	(*to MARY*) Proud of him? He was carried off to war blind drunk. (*to COOK*) And don't you look down your nose at me! If you were here you wouldn't earn enough to feed a sparrow let alone my children. I don't need your approval. Get away, Mary, and stay away from men. Grow fat, childless and self-righteous like this old maid. (*COOK slaps BETTY. The other women spring to her aid.*) You're decent folk.
BETHAN:	Betty, don't keep the men waiting.
	(*MARY and COOK leave. GRACE calls after them.*)
GRACE:	Miss! Can I be in service? Miss?!

SCENE SEVENTEEN

KING:	Do you know what I think?
WILKINS:	Not really, your Highness.
KING:	Someone has let a rat in.
WILKINS:	A rat, my Lord? How did it get in?
KING:	Perhaps I swallowed it, perhaps worse, but it's in there. (*his stomach*)
	(*The WOMEN approach the KING'S tower.*)
KATE:	The happy rat now wriggles quick
SIAN:	Squeezing through intestine.

42

GRACE: See the body writhe and billow,
Rolling to the motions of a mouth, salivating.

KATE: The rat gains power,
The face remains the same.

BETTY: The old body screams in agony,
Bloated by disorder.

KING: No!

GRACE: Gnawing, slashing, devoured and hollow.

BETTY: Now into the head of the matter,
teeth cut the scrambling brain.

EDWINA: No opposition too powerful
as the rat tears in again.

GRACE: Soon he will have consciousness.

BETTY: He will hold the power.

GRACE: In the gutter
We remain to cower

SIAN: The body hollowed
Pulls grotesque faces as the rat burrows
whining "I'm doing this for you".

WOMEN: The body will rise, erect again.
The rat, from behind glazed pain
Pulls the strings, controls the man
In accordance with the master's plan.

KING: It is! It's in me! A rat! A rat!

WILKINS: Nonsense, my Lord, I'm sure your physicians
would know if you'd swallowed a rat.

SCENE EIGHTEEN

(*The WOMEN have rushed off. They then bring on
CATHERINE DEVEREUX, the Earl of Hereford's*

daughter. They carry her aloft, throwing petals of roses as they pass. They whoop with false joy. The music is bouncy and happy. CATHERINE is bewildered.)

WILKINS: Walter! Look what I've brought you! Walter?

(Lights up on WALTER and MARY in the stable. WALTER is teaching MARY to read. She comes to the end of a sentence. Both are pleased.)

WALTER: I'll marry you.

MARY: Wait and see.

WALTER: Wait? Don't patronise me, don't dismiss my feelings. I said I'd marry you.

MARY: I'm sorry.

WALTER: I don't take this lightly, you know. I'm no fool. I know what it will mean.

WILKINS: Walter!

WALTER: I'd better go. Don't argue with me next time. It ruins it.

MARY: I'm sorry.

WALTER: Keep reading. We'll make a lady of you yet.

WILKINS: Walter!!

(WALTER runs to WILKINS.)

KING: Stop this at once!

(Everybody stops.)

KING: That's the Earl of Hereford's daughter.

WILKINS: Yes, nice girl, child-bearing hips.

KING: Hereford!

(HEREFORD appears in a special light. He snorts cocaine up a rolled banknote. He may be decadent but he has not become degenerate.)

HEREFORD: Your Majesty?

KING: You can't let this mongrel mix with our blood, our blood is pure.

HEREFORD: Some say it's past its best and turns to vinegar in our cellars.

KING: This man is a fortune hunter.

HEREFORD: I think he has no need of what I have to offer in the way of wealth, my Lord. Indeed, it is rather the other way around.

KING: These manufacturers, financiers, traders, they are shopkeepers!

HEREFORD: Your Majesty, I shall decide who my daughter shall marry and which alliance will best serve the common interests.

KING: You speak to me like this? An Earl speaks to me like a bourgeois?

HEREFORD: I have the future to be part of.

(*Lights out on HEREFORD.*)

KING: Hereford? They are deserting me.

WILKINS: As we were. (*to WALTER*) May I present Catherine Devereux?

CATHERINE: Your servant, sir.

(*WALTER exits past her to the river bank.*)

(*WOMEN of the house, in the Kitchen.*)

GILLIAN: She's beautiful. Did you see her dress?

MAGGIE: It will certainly mean a few changes.

MOLLY: What does she look like close to?

MAGGIE: Scared, I thought.

GILLIAN: Scared?

MAGGIE: Well, I suppose she has some idea of what she'll have to suffer.

GILLIAN: Oh, she'll fall in love with Master Walter, I'm sure of it.

COOK: It would certainly be a big wedding.

GILLIAN: Oh, I'd love to see it.

COOK: I wonder will Master Walter move away?

SCENE NINETEEN

(*A picnic on the river bank. WALTER sits, fed up. MARY stands away from him.*)

WALTER: Come and sit down, please. Please. (*MARY does so.*) Now, young lady, sit up, face up. What a miserable sight, lovely but miserable. (*MARY blows her nose.*) I have a complaint to make regarding your treatment of me. I have not received a single kiss all afternoon, not a brush with your hand, not a stroke of my hair. Why am I being treated this way?

MARY: I'm sorry.

WALTER: So you should be. (*pause*) I'm glad I've seen you in a bad mood. It isn't very attractive. Well? (*MARY shrugs.*) Come on! For pity's sake, Mary. I've waited all month to see you! Look what I've brought to eat.

MARY: I know what it is, I prepared it.

WALTER: Well, eat something!

MARY: No.

WALTER: Eat something!

46

MARY: No, I don't want....

WALTER: Eat, I said eat!! (*He pushes food into her mouth, smearing it on her face. She is shocked by his ferocity.*)

MARY: What did you...?

WALTER: You're like a slug today! Morbid, dull! Look at you! You're disgusting. (*MARY tries to clean her face.*) Perhaps we should just call an end to the day? Go back our separate ways.

MARY: No, please.

WALTER: (*imitates her*) No, please. Well, what do you want?

MARY: Time, a little time.

WALTER: We don't have time. If I had been in a bad mood I would have made myself change so as not to waste our precious freedom. You're being selfish and self-indulgent!

MARY: I'm sorry.

WALTER: (*imitates her*) I'm sorry.

MARY: Well, I am. You're right, you're right, you always are.

WALTER: No, I am not. What a crass and stupid thing to say about anyone.

MARY: Well, you always seem....

WALTER: Well, I'm not and don't you ever put such faith in me. I'm not wasting my time here. I wanted your love. If you can't give it I'll go.

MARY: No, please.

WALTER: Look at you.

MARY: Go then.

WALTER: I will. And that is the last time we'll meet.

MARY: Walter.

WALTER: Master.

MARY: Why are you this bitter?

WALTER: I want love, if I can't have it, why stay?

MARY: I want to love you.

WALTER: Well then, do! And don't come to me as this blubbering manifestation of self-pity.

MARY: I tried to look nice, I did try. Nothing seemed right. Please, let me hold you, please. (*She holds him. WALTER does not respond.*) Hold me. (*He does so lamely.*) I'm sorry I've let you down.

WALTER: It's yourself you've let down, Mary. I thought you had greater qualities. You've changed.

MARY: No, I haven't. I'm sick.

WALTER: Sick?

MARY: I'm expecting a child.

WALTER: What are you going to do?

MARY: There's a woman I know, a squatter. She might know what to do.

WALTER: What would she know?

MARY: How to kill it, poor thing.

WALTER: For God's sake, Mary.

MARY: What else can I do? I'll starve otherwise.

WALTER: We'll marry.

MARY: Walter, your father.

WALTER: Why not? We'll emigrate. A new country with new rules. We'll marry and I'll earn us a living.

MARY: No, you'll want your life back. You'll grow to hate and resent us.

WALTER: No, I'm proud, very proud. We'll escape.

MARY: No. It is not your child.

WALTER: You're lying.

MARY: I've been seeing the stable lad, John.

(WALTER grabs her.)

WALTER: You're lying.

MARY: Please, you can't love me, you can't.

WALTER: I do and I'm going to look after my child.

MARY: No, please, let me go.

WALTER: No. From now on you'll do as I say.

(He holds her.)

(End of ACT ONE.)

Act Two

SCENE TWENTY

(*CATHERINE and WILKINS stand in the study. CATHERINE has her back to him.*)

CATHERINE: I fear sir, your son finds no interest in me.

WILKINS: My dear, you are very wrong. He has expressed great affection for you in private to me. Give him time. He lacks grace.

CATHERINE: I shall be leaving for the season in London. Should Walter wish to pursue any arrangement with me then let it be through formal channels there. Good day.

(*She exits the stage. The WOMEN see her and come to pick her up.*)

WOMEN: Hurray!

CATHERINE: Leave me alone!

WOMEN: Ooh!

(*CATHERINE exits. MAGGIE enters the study.*)

MAGGIE: Gone already?

WILKINS: Yes.

MAGGIE: Has he told her, I mean, do you know, sir?

WILKINS: Know what?!

MAGGIE: The girl's pregnant, sir. I'm sure of it.

WILKINS: The Earl of Hereford's daughter?!

MAGGIE: No, sir. The under-cook, Mary Morgan.

WILKINS: Thank God for small mercies. Who has she told?

MAGGIE: No-one as yet but they all know. No-one will say anything, mind. They won't want to be involved.

WILKINS: They must be very frightened, Walter and the girl? I think we'll let them sweat it out. It will be a good education for them. Keep me informed, Maggie. In the meantime, send Mary Morgan to me. (*shouts*) Walter! Walter!

(*WALTER enters the study.*)

WALTER: Yes, father.

WILKINS: That will be all, Mrs Harvard.

WALTER: Must you bellow at me as if I am your dog?

WILKINS: You're quite right. I am losing my manners. It is our lack of society here, it is affecting us both adversely. I have kept you by my side out of selfish affection but now it really is time I let you go.

WALTER: Affection?

WILKINS: You are to depart to London immediately, there to arrange fresh supplies and reinforcements for the Militia. Meanwhile, you shall take in the season and meet some people of your own age and class.

WALTER: The season?! I shall be gone the whole summer. I cannot.

WILKINS: You are being timid again, Walter. Of course you can go.

WALTER: I have responsibilities here.

WILKINS: What are they?

WALTER: ...Many and varied.

WILKINS: Entrust them to me.

WALTER: No, I could not allow that.

WILKINS: I insist. Well?

WALTER: Nothing.

WILKINS: Now go and pack. I shall write to Melcroft to take charge of you.

WALTER: Melcroft! You regularly denounce him as a debauched drunkard.

WILKINS: Exactly the company a young man needs when he takes life too seriously. You shall attend Lady Catherine there but otherwise, London and all the women it has to offer are yours.

WALTER: I don't want them!

WILKINS: Walter, I swear you worry me greatly. More depends upon this and other similar marriages than you know, Walter. It is final recognition that the aristocracy needs us.

WALTER: These are times of change, Father, surely I have the...

WILKINS: Change? No, Walter, these are the times of retrenchment. We failed where the French succeeded. The time we live in is one where we appear to hark back to old values whilst we crawl on our bellies to power. Go to London, return sober and with a promise of marriage to Miss Devereux. Fail me in this and I will disinherit you of every penny. We are only trained for the exercise of authority, Walter. Without wealth we are laughable. Parrots squawking from their perch. (*He looks to the KING.*)

WALTER: Father! I...

(*MARY enters.*)

MARY: Excuse me, sir.

WILKINS: Ah, Mary.

WILKINS: Tell the cook to prepare two feasts! Walter here is off to London with Lady Catherine. He is to take up his place in the world finally. Aren't you, Walter? Well?

WALTER: Yes, father.

SCENE TWENTY-ONE

(*The KING knits. He throws the ball of wool at WIL-KINS.*)

KING: I shall come for you one day.

(*WILKINS unravels the wool as the KING needs it.*)

WILKINS: The longer the war drags on the more you come to rely on us. You shall not have the means to displace us by the time this mess is over.

KING: I wage war against agents of the devil whilst the devil sits at my table.

WILKINS: (*to himself*) Devil.

KING: Judgement will come.

WILKINS: Truth will come!

KING: What truth do you carry! Your truth is illusory.

WILKINS: No more so surely than the idea that you were put there by God to rule us. He may be mysterious but he's not irresponsible. The truth is that you clutch at blades of grass whilst we've built towns and cities to encircle you. We are wealth.

KING: This is my country!

WILKINS: To you land is wealth. When one field fails so does yours. What hope have you to offer a starving man? I can at least offer him a loan from my bank.

KING: That's it, you see. You loan money to those who cannot repay the debt. Your wealth is illusory!

WILKINS: Of course it is! But if I own a debt, I own the man. If he fails me and starves I take his land. I am doing no less for you.

KING: The rat steals me from the inside. This is treason.

WILKINS: Not at all. We'll let your family stay on as a curiosity in our shop window. You'll thank me. It's better than peasants chopping heads off. They might make a mistake and chop mine off, then where would you be?

KING: I'll come for you, crush you!

SCENE TWENTY-TWO

(*Lights up on the shanty town. The WOMEN wash soldiers' shirts. As GRACE takes one from BETTY to hang up, BETHAN snatches it from her and throws it on the ground in front of BETTY.*)

BETHAN: It's dirty. Wash it again.

(*After a tense pause, GRACE steps forward to pick it up.*)

BETHAN: Not you! (*GRACE stops.*) (*to BETTY*) Pick it up. Pick it up or get thrown out of the camp like your mother. I wonder what's happened to her, eh? Pick it up.

(*Eventually, BETTY picks up the shirt and begins*

washing it again. Lights up simultaneously on the river bank where HEFINA and SARAH sit, exhausted.)

SARAH: Look at the water, Hefina. Like a golden road paved with silks and satins.

HEFINA: Yes.

SARAH: I think it's going to London.

HEFINA: What is?

SARAH: The road. We should follow it. I bet we'd find my children there. That's where they'll be, sitting with the King.

HEFINA: Yes, Sarah, that's where they'll be all right.

SARAH: You think so? I think so, I've got a good feeling about this. I'll send them my hat, they'll know then, always had this hat.

HEFINA: Don't throw it....

SARAH: There it goes. They'll know I'm alive now then. I'll follow the river to London. Get back with my children. That's what you should do, Hefina. Go back to Betty. She'll be missing you.

(HEFINA sings. The shanty town WOMEN join the song on the second verse, moving through the audience towards the river bank.)

HEFINA: Some tell of a world turned upside down
I would not believe it of this town
For those in power are those with vested ways
They are there while the poor one pays.

Some tell of a world turned upside down
I will not live to see this world turn around.
Oh, my girl, I've done what I can do,
Now I leave the turning up to you.

Some say there is a world turned upside down
But I do not know how to turn that axis round
But if I could for my daughter, this I'd do
Take up arms against the mighty few.

The future's in my daughter's hands
To make of it what e're she can.
I'll say to her, and without fear
Take the world by the hair, my dear.

You will find in the world turned upside down
A place where a childhood can be found
Together you'll be a central piece
In the central peace
Of the world turned upside down.

SARAH: I'm going now. I'm not waiting.

HEFINA: What are you doing?!

SARAH: I'm going to join my children.

HEFINA: Sarah, no! Don't! Come back!

(*SARAH leaps into the river/arms of the shanty town WOMEN. They carry her aloft as if she is drowning. As the sound dies away, HEFINA collapses.*)

HEFINA: You bitch.

KING: When the bough breaks the cradle will fall
Down will come baby, cradle and all.

SCENE TWENTY -THREE

(*MARY carries a basket of wood past white sheets hanging in the yard. She stops for breath.*)

JOHN: (*carrying herbs*) Mary. (*She looks, says nothing.*)

You're with child.

MARY: Leave...

JOHN: Come on! I know you are. Is it mine? (*She spits at his feet.*) Wait! These herbs. I had a word with my mother. It's all right, I didn't say who they was for. These herbs, they'll get rid of it. Well, maybe.

MARY: No!

JOHN: Mary! If it's mine, marry me. I'll look after you. If it t'ain't then by God, girl, take these herbs. Make a brew, that's all. Take em! And best take them quick, girl.

MARY: No.

JOHN: What will become of you?

MARY: I'm going to a new country, new rules.

JOHN: There ain't no such place, girl. Not for you. (*MARY exits.*) Does he know? Where is he, eh? Ain't here to look after you! (*JOHN, sad and angry, exits.*)

SCENE TWENTY-FOUR

(*MARY goes into the kitchen and grabbing a shawl, makes for the shanty town.*)

MARY: Excuse me. I'm looking for a friend of mine, Hefina Pugh.

GRACE: Where'd you get your dress?

MARY: From my master.

GRACE: I want one.

MARY: Well.

GRACE: Take me back with you. I'll be like you.

MARY: I'm afraid I can't do that. Do you know Betty? Can you take me to her?

GRACE: Why should I tell you?

MARY: Please, I feel faint. Let me sit. Here?

BETHAN: *(to GRACE)* What's the matter with her, Grace? Well? Talking to you's like trying to see in the dark. *(to MARY)* She's a quill with no ink, this one. You all right, girl?

MARY: I'll be fine.

BETHAN: Then you'll be on your way?

MARY: Perhaps. I want to see Betty.

BETHAN: What's that about then?

MARY: Nothing.

          (BETTY enters.)

BETHAN: You faint, did you? What, don't they feed you up there?

MARY: They feed us.

BETHAN: They feed you but you can't keep it down, that it?

BETTY: Leave her alone.

BETHAN: You're pregnant, girl. Think I can't tell? Master's brat, is it? I'll do you a good job, girl, fair price.

BETTY: Leave her!

BETHAN: What else you going to get? You'll be safe. I've got rid of dozens, could do it now if you wanted.

MARY: No!

          (MARY makes to leave but BETTY stops her and holds her firmly in her arms.)

BETTY: How many months?

MARY: Nearly seven.

BETTY: God, girl, you're tiny for seven months. Does the father know?

MARY: Yes.

BETTY: Who is he then, this lad of yours?

MARY: It's Walter Wilkins.

BETTY: That bastard!

MARY: What's he done to you?

BETTY: He brought the Militia in here! Horse-whipped a daft old woman, then rode over her. They gave us a choice, whoring or the Parish. I chose whoring. Hefina made a run for it. She'll have been picked up or starved by now. I thought she'd come back. Now we're all prisoners. Lie down, let me feel for the baby. (*MARY does so.*)

MARY: Can you help me?

BETTY: What, abort it? No, girl, you can't do that. It's too late.

MARY: Too late?

BETTY: Messing with it now, it could kill you. We've had women die here because of it. Listen, best way by far is to birth naturally then kill it. Listen, listen. Think what's best. You birth it, then kill it before it wakes. It won't know nothing. You won't even look into its eyes. Just do it. And quickly. That way, if you're lucky, you'll live. Don't tell me you still love him?

MARY: Master Walter? I don't... I don't know.

BETHAN: Hey, girl, you put your faith in old Bethan. I'll do you a special price, special price.

(*GRACE stops MARY and hands her a knife.*)

GRACE: I could be your daughter.

(*MARY runs away.*)

KING: Rock a bye baby
         On the tree top
         When the wind blows
         The cradle will rock.

         Oh. I hear their suffering, the wailing of mothers
         laying their children into the ground. Children,
         children stand at a place where all roads cross.
         And where the traffic from any direction may
         strike them down.

         Rock a bye baby
         On the tree top
         When the wind blows
         The cradle will rock.

SCENE TWENTY-FIVE

*(WILKINS blows hunting bugle. Festivities commence.
HEREFORD, WALTER and CATHERINE are
escorted by the shanty town WOMEN past MARY,
who watches from the kitchen with GILLIAN.)*

GILLIAN: Master Walter's back! He's brought her home!
            Isn't it romantic?!

WILKINS: Walter, my dear, dear boy. *(he hugs WALTER)*
            Catherine. Come inside, you must be tired. I have
            had prepared a wonderful engagement dinner!
            *(CATHERINE enters. WILKINS stops WALTER
            fiercely.)* There's just the question of Mary
            Morgan's bastard to deal with now. *(WALTER is
            shocked that WILKINS knows.)* Make sure nothing
            embarrassing happens. Tell the girl to be discreet!

            *(He leaves WALTER on the steps to the study and
            turns to his guests. WALTER stays looking up. The
            actors on stage freeze and their light goes down as*

MARY approaches WALTER.)

MARY: Master Walter.

WALTER: Go away.

MARY: No one can see.

WALTER: Go away.

MARY: I did like you said. I've carried it.

           (WALTER looks at her.)

WALTER: Get rid of it.

MARY: I can't.

WALTER: You must.

MARY: It's too late.

WALTER: Get rid of it! You don't understand. We can't have the child now. We can't. *(pause)*

MARY: No.

WALTER: We must... bide our time. See how things work out. It's very difficult for me at the moment.

MARY: Yes.

WALTER: We'll be together, somehow, maybe not how we'd planned, but together.

MARY: You'll look after me?

WALTER: I promise. *(MARY breaks down.)* Look, please, don't, if someone sees.

MARY: To hell with you!

           (WALTER grabs her roughly.)

WALTER: Now you listen to me?! *(MARY has a contraction.)* What is it?

MARY: The child. It's been like this all night and morning. I'm scared, Walter. I think it's coming.

WALTER: You can't. Not today, you can't!

MARY: What am I going to do?

WALTER: Get away from here, hide. Go home.

MARY: I can't go home, they don't know.

WALTER: Well, think of something! I don't know, do I?

            (*COOK exits from kitchen and calls. She does not see MARY or WALTER.*)

COOK: Mary? Mary? Where are you? There's work to be done! Typical, dinner to prepare and she's off moping.

            (*COOK goes back into the kitchen.*)

MARY: I want you there, when it happens.

WALTER: What?! You must be insane.

MARY: I'm not doing it. It's your child, you kill it.

WALTER: Mary! ...I can't.

MARY: You must. You can't leave it to me.

WALTER: I'm not doing it and I'm not going to be there! Do you want to ruin everything? Supposing I was discovered? Eh? What then? Mary, I love you. I will look after you but I cannot do this, not today. (*Long pause. The contraction passes.*) Has it stopped?

MARY: It'll be back. What will I say to them? (*WALTER has no answer.*) Still got your knife? Give it me. (*WALTER hands her the pen-knife he used on the picnic. MARY is making WALTER part of this.*)

MARY: (*getting up*) Nothing, nothing to say?

WALTER: I'm sorry. I'll shower you with gifts, anything you want.

MARY: Kiss me... I've missed you so much.

WALTER: (*His image of her is now distasteful.*) I can't. (*MARY *sadly turns, aware of how loathsome she is, conceals the knife and walks away.*) I do love you.

(*WILKINS comes to the edge of the study.*)

WILKINS: Come and join us, Walter.

(*WALTER looks up at him. Lights down.*)

SCENE TWENTY-SIX

(*Kitchen. Molly scrubs a bloody meat block. MARY enters.*)

COOK: Well?

MARY: Sorry.

COOK: Finish that block. Molly, clean down the table. We've a very important meal to prepare! (*MARY stares at the blood.*) Get a move on! (*MARY starts scrubbing the block. She gets another contraction whilst COOK speaks.*) I'll need pastry enough for the large dish. Mary, do it. Molly, get fresh sugar from the stores. I'll need three pound of apples doing, fetch them whilst you're there. Take from the top shelf first, they've been wrapped long enough and treat them like china.

(*MOLLY has noticed MARY in pain. The blood is making MARY ill. MOLLY nudges the COOK to stop her.*)

Mary? You still hurting?

(*MARY nods.*)

MARY: Cramps. I think I'd best go lie down.

COOK: You can't, not today.

MARY: I think it's best.

(*pause*)

COOK: Go then. I'll get someone in. I'll bring some soup up in a while, see how you are.

(*MARY goes. MOLLY is concerned for her.*)

MOLLY: Is this it?

COOK: I don't know what you're talking about.

MOLLY: We can't leave her alone. She needs help.

COOK: We've left her alone till now, Molly! She's not the only woman in the house who's done this. I can't afford to make it my business and for sure you can't either. Whatever that girl decides to do is hers alone to know about. Now, you stay out of it.

MOLLY: But, Mary....

COOK: That's the last we speak of it! Now, I'm going to have to get Maggie Harvard to help in here and I don't want her to know anything.

SCENE TWENTY-SEVEN

(*MARY'S bedroom. We see MARY taking off the top of her dress. She wears a cotton undergarment which is bound by cloth to suppress the pregnancy. She is terrified, moving deliberately, concentrated upon her task. She gags herself and begins releasing her stomach by unwinding the bandages. Lights out.*)

SCENE TWENTY-EIGHT

(*Lights up on WILKINS'S study.*)

WILKINS: But the King will insist upon pursuing his bill against the Company.

HEREFORD: Even if it passes through the Commons, I can muster enough support in the Lords to water it down and delay it.

WILKINS: By the way, the Company has made your family a present of a share in Chittagong, by way of celebrating this forthcoming marriage.

HEREFORD: (*To CATHERINE and WALTER*) Isn't that splendid?

C&W: Yes, splendid.

SCENE TWENTY-NINE

(*Kitchen. MAGGIE, COOK and GILLIAN bustle about.*)

MAGGIE: Right, let me take a look at you. (*She checks GILLIAN.*) Cook?

COOK: Very good.

(*MOLLY enters with a bowl of soup.*)

MAGGIE: Aren't you changed yet? I need you upstairs.

MOLLY: I couldn't get into the room.

COOK: Didn't Mary hear you?

MOLLY: I called to her. I couldn't push the door open.

MAGGIE: Perhaps she's unconscious.

COOK: No, I'm sure she's just sleeping. She's a sound sleeper.

GILLIAN: Perhaps she's fallen asleep against the door?

MAGGIE: Why yes, Gillian, that must be it. Unless of course something's going on? What is it?

COOK: A fever, that's all.

MAGGIE: I'm going to see for myself.

COOK: We haven't time. Serve the food, the Master's waiting.

MAGGIE: Let them wait!

COOK: Maggie!

(*MAGGIE exits pursued by COOK and MOLLY trying to stop her.*)

SCENE THIRTY

(*Spotlights up on Wilkins's study, illuminating WALTER. CATHERINE appears behind him and in slow motion places her hands over his eyes as the WOMEN pass. They stay in this posture.*)

SCENE THIRTY-ONE

(*Lights up on MARY on her bed. She sits upright with her knees up looking at the baby which is lying upon the bed. She is fascinated by it, totally exhausted. She no longer wears the gag. A confusion of emotions emerge through her delirium. She is gentle with the baby. The baby is mimed. The child must open its eyes in the mind of the actress. MARY stares, falling in love with the baby.*)

MAGGIE: Mary Morgan! Mary Morgan!

COOK: For pity's sake, Maggie!

MAGGIE: Open the door!

(MARY lets out a cry like the baby's, takes Walter's knife and slashes the child's throat.)

MAGGIE: Open it! Open it! You're the devil, the devil! Mary Morgan, open this door! Open it! *(MARY pulls blankets over the child.)*

MARY: What is it? What's the matter?

COOK: It's alright, Mary.

MOLLY: Don't open it!

MAGGIE: *(pushes MOLLY brutally aside)* If she's done anything there'll be a trial, your words will be remembered, my girl. Open the door!

MARY: All right, all right! I'm just ill, that's all. Leave me alone.

(MARY pulls the bed away from the door. MAGGIE bursts in. They know from MARY'S appearance what has happened.)

MAGGIE: You witch! You've killed it! You think I've suffered humiliations all my life so that you can just do it the easy way? You're wrong, there's a price to pay in this life. You'll pay it, you'll pay it. You can't take life into your own hands. You're evil!

MARY: No, no, leave it. It's mine, leave it...

(MAGGIE pulls back the sheets and they see the dead baby.)

SCENE THIRTY-TWO

(Meanwhile, in WILKINS'S study WALTER jumps as

if CATHERINE has just this second placed her hands over his eyes. CATHERINE takes her hands away. They laugh at WALTER'S shock.)

KING: Without clear rule the people know not how to behave. My cloak! I go out today! They have need of me.

SCENE THIRTY-THREE

(*WILKINS and HEREFORD have left the study.*)

CATHERINE:Do you know this awful girl?

WALTER: Catherine, we must leave this place. When we marry, leave this place to my father.

CATHERINE: Yes, yes please. We shall be free of him. You will be happy. I will have it no other way. He shall not rule you. That is my promise. Oh my poor boy. Don't let this wretched girl upset you. Sweet thing. (*She kisses him.*)

SCENE THIRTY-FOUR

(*MARY'S bedroom. MAGGIE, HEREFORD and WILKINS discuss the "case".*)

HEREFORD:Get her to the jail, insist upon it!

WILKINS: They won't take her in this condition! Ridiculous! Get her back to health so that they can hang her. Bureaucracy gone mad! Look, with any luck she'll die here.

HEREFORD:And if she doesn't this will go to court! When is the next circuit?

WILKINS: We've just missed one. There isn't another until the spring.

HEREFORD: Six months! Then the engagement is postponed. If any of this should cause a stain upon Walter's character, it will make the marriage indefensible, you understand that?

WILKINS: Hardinge will try the case. I'll have him, don't you worry. Walter will be as pure as snow.

HEREFORD: Then be sure he makes no more stupid mistakes. Giving her his knife was grossly incompetent.

WILKINS: I will take charge.

HEREFORD: Secure a hanging, Wilkins, nothing less will do. This girl must be silenced. I will inform my daughter that for the time being the arrangements are postponed. (*HEREFORD goes.*)

WILKINS: Maggie, clean the girl up, feed her little, perhaps this affair will never come to trial.

(*MAGGIE is now subdued, torn by her actions.*)

MAGGIE: No, I'll not do that for you. She's suffered enough.

WILKINS: Don't be absurd, woman.

(*WILKINS exits.*)

SCENE THIRTY-FIVE

KING: Bring my crown, my cross to bear! Today we shall go out and administer to the weak the justice of our Lord!

WILKINS: Going backwards seems to have helped your Majesty!

KING: Indeed! I sense the dawn retreating before me!

SCENE THIRTY-SIX

(*WOMEN of the shanty town.*)

HEFINA: (*standing apart*) A hard winter. Stone against skin.

SARAH: (*standing apart*) A freezing. Shards of ice cut light into the gloom. The sky plays patterns on the surface, tempting us to rise up into the light.

HEFINA: An ice without compassion.

WOMEN: Burn it.

SCENE THIRTY-SEVEN

(*WILKINS'S study.*)

WILKINS: All I am trying to do is protect your reputation.

WALTER: And for that she must hang?

WILKINS: Your only thought should be for Catherine, young man. She, after all, is innocent! You must write to Mary Morgan, tell her that if she confesses to the murder you will enter a plea to Judge Hardinge.

WALTER: A plea?

WILKINS: That you will take her into your custody and guarantee her future good behaviour, something along those lines. Tell her Hardinge will agree only if he knows nothing of your affair. It is therefore imperative that she conceals your part in all this.

WALTER: And then what?

WILKINS: Then, Walter, she will keep quiet in the belief that it will save her neck.

WALTER: She does not deserve my treachery.

WILKINS: Oh, really? You believed her when she told you that she loved you, that you were all she ever wanted.

WALTER: I believed that she loved me, yes, yes! I believe I know the difference between love and what you offer.

WILKINS: Kent! Kent, come in here. (*to WALTER*) I thought you might.

            (*JOHN KENT enters nervously.*)

WALTER: What is he to do with this?

WILKINS: Tell him what you told me. Tell him.

JOHN: Well, sir, I....

WILKINS: Tell him!

JOHN: I had it with Mary Morgan, sir, in the stables.

WILKINS: Did she encourage you?

JOHN: Yes, sir, oh yes.

WILKINS: When was this?

JOHN: Up until she were pregnant, sir, then it stopped between us.

WILKINS: Was it your child she killed?

JOHN: Couldn't say, sir.

WILKINS: No, indeed and neither can Walter. Get out, Kent. (*KENT goes. Silence.*) Walter, I would not see you harmed in any way. Forgive me? We have all been fools in love, even I. Now only your duty remains, to make well this awful wound you have opened in all our lives.

WALTER: I don't know how all this happened. I'm sorry.

WOMEN: An ice without compassion. Burn it!

SCENE THIRTY-EIGHT

(*Lights up on MARY and HEFINA huddled together in the prison cell. HEFINA is asleep. MARY reads the letter from WALTER. SARAH is illuminated as a ghost on the river bank and remains until the end of the play.*)

HEFINA: Rise up to the surface...

(*HEFINA is crushed, beaten, down and out.*)

MARY: You were dreaming.

(*No response. HEFINA shuffles away from MARY. MARY moves beside her for warmth. HEFINA stares at her.*)

MARY: Keep warm. From Presteigne, aren't you? Betty's mother. Rub your hands. Don't you remember me? Mary Morgan.

(*MARY rubs HEFINA'S hands.*)

HEFINA: (*takes her hands away*) Think maybe this Winter will kill me off.

MARY: No.

HEFINA: Why not?

MARY: Because it won't.

(*HEFINA pushes MARY away. MARY fights back and cuddles HEFINA. They rock each other for comfort.*)

HEFINA: I know what you did. (*MARY stops rocking.*) In this world we plunge the dagger into our own hearts all the time, girl. (*She now holds MARY.*) Anyone would think we all hated ourselves. Perhaps we do in the end. I think we might.

MARY: Others still love us, I'm sure.

HEFINA: I don't know.

MARY: They do.

HEFINA: There ain't no young master in shiny boots going
           to come for you, girl. Best kill that hope in you as
           well. (*MARY stands and moves away from HEFINA.*)
           There ain't no-one who won't kill if they have to.

SCENE THIRTY-NINE

(*The KING is dressed in his robe.*)

KING: To Presteigne my justice comes! The trial of
           worlds clashing.

           (*The WOMEN of the shanty town wheel the tower
           around the auditorium. A great pagan celebration as
           the entry of Hardinge into Presteigne is re-enacted. The
           tower comes to a halt opposite WILKINS'S study. The
           curtains gather at the waist to reveal HARDINGE.
           HEREFORD, WALTER and WILKINS face HARD-
           INGE from the study.*)

HARDINGE: A splendid reception as usual, Mr Wilkins.

KING: We're very grateful.

WILKINS: What does it take to get a hanging verdict from a
           judge these days?!

HARDINGE: I beg your pardon?

WILKINS: Two weeks ago in Brecon you let a woman off for
           killing her illegitimate child!

HARDINGE: The jury did not find her guilty.

KING: Was she guilty?

HARDINGE: Of course she was. It is a common offence, your
           Majesty, and may I say nowhere more common
           than in Mr Wilkins's constituency.

WILKINS: I hope you're not suggesting that I am responsible for this Mary Morgan being without God?

HEREFORD: Gentlemen, the trial, can we speak amongst ourselves.

BETTY: They're going to stitch her up.

GRACE: Gentry sticks together.

HARDINGE: Call Mary Morgan!

(*MARY leaves the cell and comes to stand before HARDINGE and the KING.*)

HARDINGE: Mary Morgan, you are charged that on September 23rd, you did murder your own child.

WILKINS: George, the Company faces a major challenge in the Commons. If the King's bill goes through many people who for now support the war and the King will put money elsewhere. Money that might lose us both the war and the King.

KING: What is he saying? Speak up!

HARDINGE: Are these your republican opinions, Wilkins?

WILKINS: Mathematical fact is what they are, George. Hereford and I can oppose the bill by broadening ownership amongst those who will vote for us. But many members of both Houses will not be convinced that opposition to the King is in their interests unless they see that we are the future, not him.

HEREFORD: The marriage of Walter and Catherine is essential proof that we mean to be the future, George.

HARDINGE: Naturally, I want what is best for the King.

WILKINS: Then the marriage must happen.

HEREFORD: George, if this scandalous and ungodly act were to be in any way associated with young Walter here, the marriage would lose credibility.

WILKINS: We want to make sure that she says nothing in court, there must be no record of her defence counsel, then we want her hung.

HARDINGE: I cannot do this! The Jury find her guilty or innocent, I can only pass sentence. Surely you can persuade her to keep quiet?

WILKINS: She is notoriously indiscreet.

HEREFORD: George, when the bill comes to the Commons we need someone with eloquence and wit to oppose it.

WILKINS: It will be your greatest performance.

HEREFORD: History in the making.

WILKINS: And you can name your own price.

HEREFORD: We need you, George.

KING: I can't hear... has the trial started?

HARDINGE: One moment, your Majesty.

WILKINS: You'll take centre stage, George, where you should be.

HARDINGE: Well, young man, are you not going to enter a plea on behalf of this girl? (*to WALTER*)

WALTER: What she has done is against God, that is beyond my pleading or opinion surely.

HEREFORD: Well said, Walter.

HARDINGE: Well, my fine young fellow, so be it. But I leave it up to you. I shall not pass judgement until I hear your pain ringing in my ears!

WILKINS: We've said, you keep Walter out of it.

HARDINGE: Oh no, you will be right in the heart of it, my boy. You'll be on the jury.

HEREFORD: Are you insane, Hardinge?!

KING: I hope not.

WILKINS: No, what better proof of Walter's innocence than for him to sit in judgement. It is beyond belief that he could be so callous.

WALTER: You can't be serious.

HARDINGE:Oh, I am. I'll watch the verdict sound forth from your lips and know my part in this shall remain sealed by them. You shall lead the jury towards a guilty verdict. The guilt then is yours alone to live with. Do you understand me? I can only pass sentence of death if *you* find her guilty.

WILKINS: Which you will, Walter.

HEREFORD: Which you will.

KING: Well? What has been decided?

HARDINGE:We shall hear the evidence.

WILKINS: (*to HEREFORD*) Good. I thought for a moment we'd have to threaten to say the child was Hardinge's.

          (*WALTER descends the study stage to sit beneath HARDINGE. COOK, MAGGIE and MOLLY speak in unison.*)

C, M&M: Mary Morgan was taken ill continuing her work till near one o'clock when she went to bed. At half past seven we were unable to gain access to her room.

KING: Wait, wait, wait! Why are they all speaking in unison?

HARDINGE:Their statements are identical, my Lord. I thought it would save time.

KING: That's rather an odd coincidence, isn't it?

HARDINGE:Continue.

C, M&M: Upon entering the room Mary Morgan was

charged with having delivered herself of a child. With bitter oaths she eventually owned up to the child which was in the under bed, cut open among the feathers with the head nearly divided from the body, supposed by a penknife.

WILKINS: Hm hm.

(*HARDINGE points at the WOMEN.*)

C, M&M: A knife which was under the same bed. Witness the marks of Elizabeth Evelyn, Margaret Harvard, Molly Meredith.

MARY: I had to kill it, I couldn't let it go to the parish, poor thing.

BETTY: Let he who is without guilt cast the first stone!

HEFINA: When a child lives in squalor you desert them, when they break your laws only then do you want them!

GRACE: The child, what was it?

MARY: A girl, like you.

(*GRACE stands by MARY and holds her hand.*)

HARDINGE: How does the jury find?

(*WALTER waits to pronounce the verdict.*)

MARY: A new country, new rules. One word and we're on our way, Walter.

WALTER: Guilty.

(*Uproar amongst the WOMEN.*)

HARDINGE: Stop this disorder! I will clear the court!

KING: Are you so far down the path of depravity that you cannot see this jury has found justly? Hardinge, continue.

HEREFORD: This could turn to riot.

WILKINS: I've brought in fresh troops with cannon, shot and

musket enough to shoot the entire population. I am prepared.

HARDINGE: Mary Morgan, upon evidence which leaves not a shade of doubt upon the mind, you are convicted of murdering your child, a newborn infant of your own sex, the offspring of your secret and vicious love. You could not hate the victim of this murder, it never offended you.

Had it lived you might have lost your place, you might have lived in poverty as well as shame, but was this a reason to kill it? At your wild and youthful age, undisciplined by fear, and with such early habits of depraved self-indulgence, it is not probable that a religion, which breathes in every page of it the love to infants, could have been impressed upon your mind.

To cut off a young creature like you in the morning of her day is an affliction thrown upon me which I have no power to describe, or to bear so well as perhaps I should.

You must not think we are cruel. It is to save other infants like yours and many other girls like you, from the pit into which you are fallen.

You are to be taken from this place...

(*Uproar in court.*)

BETTY: Mary, we've sent for a reprieve. A rider has set off for London and the King. He'll be back in three days.

(*WILKINS indicates to HARDINGE to do something.*)

HARDINGE: The execution will be brought forward to tomorrow! Now disperse! Disperse! Wilkins, call in the troops!

(*WILKINS raises his arm, lighting now just on HARDINGE and MARY.*)

SCENE FORTY

MARY: Why are you doing this to me? What have I done that you haven't asked of me?

HARDINGE:Mary, you cannot seek answers from this world but from the next. You must prepare yourself for death.

MARY: How? What do I do?

HARDINGE:You have committed a foul sin, surely you realise that?

MARY: People are killed in many ways, why blame me so? Did I not do what was expected of me?

HARDINGE:It was your individual choice, Mary, no-one else's. You alone must atone to God. Life is sacred, Mary. That is absolute, it has to be. Society would tear itself apart if it were not so, God would not want that. Repent and confess your sins.

MARY: I will do. What will happen?

HARDINGE:He who is a loving father to us all shall surely find mercy. There is a place of green pastures and abundance where you may rest with your child and in loving example earn the forgiveness of our father.

MARY: I'll earn it, I'll work hard. Give me the chance to prove it to you.

HARDINGE:You must seek it from God, not from me. You are beyond my help, Mary. In the morning you shall hang, there is no other course.

MARY: No, I see. They want me dead, don't they? All this rush. God, I beg you, let me in. If you give me the chance I will love it in your land of abundance and will, if you let me, pour love onto that little girl. I am evil. I am. I don't understand how I came to be, but please forgive me.

HARDINGE: Be in peace, Mary.

MARY: Is Master Walter coming to see me? (*HARDINGE turns and looks at her.*) Well then, tell him I'm going to a new country with new rules.

SCENE FORTY-ONE

WILKINS: Bring out the prisoner!

BETTY: You don't take her on our cart!

WILKINS: You've been paid, you'll take her.

BETTY: Keep your money. First man touches my horse, I'll whip him raw.

WILKINS: Stand aside or be shot, we'll pull the cart! Get her to the gallows.

(*MARY walks and climbs onto a cart. BETHAN, the SERGEANT, HEREFORD and WILKINS pull it around the hall, ending at the gallows. The WOMEN from the house and town hum HEFINA'S song and turn their backs on the cart as it passes them.*)

HEREFORD: Where's the hangman?

WILKINS: He's refused to hang her.

HEREFORD: Who'll hang her?

BETHAN: I'll do it, sir, I'll do it.

(*BETHAN volunteers. She goes to put a blindfold on MARY.*)

MARY: No. I shall see this place and its people as I die.

BETHAN: She's too light, she won't hang.

WILKINS: What?

BETHAN: Ain't enough weight left on her.

HEREFORD: A shilling. Hang onto her.

> (*HEREFORD pays BETHAN a shilling. WALTER approaches MARY. Kneeling, he wraps his arms around her and lays his head against her stomach. MARY makes as if to stroke his hair. Her neck is broken. She collapses into WALTER'S arms, laying across his lap.*)

HEREFORD: Welcome to the family, Walter.

> (*HEREFORD exits.*)

WILKINS: I want the body removed. It might become a shrine for these women.

> (*WILKINS exits the study.*)

HARDINGE: It will be taken to London to be dissected.

WILKINS: Excellent.

> (*The WOMEN of the house and shanty town enter and take MARY'S body from WALTER.*)

BETTY: Quickly now, take the body to the church. The Rector has agreed to bury her in his garden. But be quick before Wilkins finds out.

WILKINS: What of the other prisoner (*re: HEFINA*)?

HARDINGE: Two year's hard labour.

WILKINS: Dinner?

HARDINGE: I'm leaving tonight. May God have mercy on us all. (*HEREFORD and WILKINS tie a blindfold over HARDINGE'S eyes.*)

HEREFORD: We'll be in touch, George.

> (*HEREFORD leaves. WILKINS enters his study. BETHAN stands beneath him.*)

SCENE FORTY-TWO

BETTY: Bethan!

(BETHAN is terrified as the WOMEN of the town surround her with twisted sheets.)

SIAN: Steal the milk from my baby, Cuckoo King.

GRACE: Rob me of sight, of hearing, of taste, of touch, of expectation.

KING: What are these women doing?

KATE: We'll mop his brow and let him steal our warmth.

EDWINA: Absorb our heat and shiver in his shadow.

HEFINA: Set a funeral pyre.

GRACE: Ask the King where the war is, Bethan.

KING: Wilkins!

WILKINS: Your Majesty?

KING: Stop them.

SARAH: Rise up into the light.

(The WOMEN have sheets, they capture BETHAN and wrap them around her neck. BETTY has a petrol can and spills it over the sheets to make them burn. An image akin to 'necklacing'.)

KING: Wilkins! Stop them. Please.

(WILKINS rushes and climbs the scaffolding tower.)

WILKINS: Of course, your Majesty. I'm coming.

SARAH: Rise up to the surface.

(The WOMEN are about to torch BETHAN.)

WILKINS: Bring in the troops!

(The WOMEN turn to see the soldiers and freeze.)

KING: Thank you. We are indebted to you.

WILKINS: Indeed, your Majesty, you are.

           (*The KING slumps back onto his throne, fearful of WILKINS. WILKINS smiles.*)

KING: Now we see you.

WILKINS: The world changes!

           (*Lights out on a triumphant WILKINS.*)

           (*THE END.*)

Tarzanne

Tarzanne was originally commissioned by Theatr Powys for the Mid Powys Youth Theatre and was performed at the Wyeside Arts Centre, Builth Wells, in October 1988. The production was jointly directed by Greg Cullen and Guy Roderick, with Musical Direction by Clive Fishlock and Choreography by Rachel Freeman. The script was rewritten for a joint touring production by Theatr Powys and Footloose Dance Company in 1990, directed by Martin Jameson with Musical Direction by Matthew Bailey and Design by Janis Hart. Greg Cullen rewrote the entire play for the Mid Powys Youth Theatre in 1995 for performance by them at the Wyeside Arts Centre. This production was directed by Greg Cullen, with Musical Direction by Paula Gardiner, Choreography by Rachel Freeman, Design by Meri Wells and Steve Mattison, Costume Design by Allie Saunders. It is this script which is published here.

The Chimpanzees

It is essential that whoever produces this play makes sure the actors correctly perform the chimpanzee movements. There are a set of simple rules which when adhered to make the illusion quite stunning. See the Acknowledgements for advice. I recommend that any producer look at the work of Jane Goodall who has studied chimpanzees in the wild for over thirty years. National Geographic have also produced a video of her work studying the chimpanzees of Gombe. Understanding the individuality of the chimpanzees, their society and pre-occupation with status will illuminate the entire play, including the human interactions.

I have given stage directions for the chimpanzee scenes. These were devised in rehearsal. However, apart from the obvious plot points, a director may well wish to devise new sequences based upon the characters that the company evolves for the chimpanzees. Some chimpanzees, such as Adam, Ben and Alice have key roles, otherwise actors can develop characters themselves. Adam is the Alpha (head) male until deposed by Ben. Adam protects Anne. He is a just king. Ben is a psychopath whose lust for blood is based upon the relationship between a mother and daughter at Gombe called Pom and Passion. The other chimpanzees are very wary of him. Alice is based upon Flo, a chimpanzee at Gombe who was an affectionate and playful mother. It is better to stylize the chimpanzee makeup and costume as attempts to be naturalistic will inevitably fail. We looked for personality, facial expression, body shape and the movement qualities in the costume.

Scenes are sometimes simultaneously played, although for clarity in the script scenes are numbered separately. The set therefore needs to be multi-locational. The action of the play cannot wait for set changes, it must flow. The original production was in Promenade, the second, Traverse. The third production was 'End On', consisting of a greenhouse which doubled as the jungle camp. Stages left and right allowed for separate interior and exterior locations. The centre stage could be seen as an interior in the stately home, exterior gardens or jungle. 'Trees' were suggested by poles pitched at angles towards the roof, set within these were platforms for the chimpanzees to use and for human characters in more stylised scenes. A multitude of levels allow the physicality of the chimpanzees to be fully exploited. A huge cargo net was flown from the balcony to the trees on stage, allowing the chimpanzees to travel over the audience's heads. A jungle watering hole doubled as a pond in the garden.

TARZANNE

CHARACTERS

Humans

A Music Hall artiste.
A Music Hall actor dressed in a chimpanzee suit.

Anne Brecknor
Lady Valerie Brecknor (Anne's paternal grandmother)
Elizabeth Goodwithy (her companion)
Geoffrey Brecknor (Anne's father)
Ruth Brecknor (Anne's mother)
Augusta (Lady Valerie's niece)
Timothy (Augusta's son)
Sophie (Augusta's daughter)

A (white) hunter

Jenkins (Head Gardener)
Dewey Jenkins (his son)
Jacqueline (a maid)
Mrs Hardwick (Anne's governess)

Chimpanzees

Adam (Alpha male)
Alice (Alpha female)
Autumn (Alice's baby who is killed by Ruth Brecknor)
Bruno (Alice's son)
Bessie (Alice's daughter)
Ben (A psychopath)
Busta (A harassed mother)

Other chimpanzees were created by the actors and the number of them can expand or contract as required. The first letter of their name indicates their status within the colony, 'A' being the highest. Our lowest status chimp was called Friday.

It is possible to cast the play with human characters doubling as chimpanzees — with the exception of Anne. The doubling should develop meaning in the play, for example Timothy should double with Ben.

Elephants

A Mother
Her baby

The Mother elephant was created by using stilts on the actor's arms and legs. The baby stood on the ground, but held small stilts in her hands. Plastic brewer's tubing was hidden in the trunks so that water could be sucked up and sprayed back out.

Act One

SCENE ONE

(The story is set imprecisely within the Victorian era, where feudal and capitalist relations between classes co-exist uncomfortably. The human characters need a stylised costume which comments upon the restrictions of human society and the transformation of our shape. The chimpanzees need to master the techniques of chimpanzee movement and to understand their society and development. Their costume should not attempt to be realistic (no hairy monkey suits, please). Nor should masks be used. Suggestions of chimpanzee physique, age, character, status and qualities of movement would be helpful. A respect for their individuality is important.

Audience preset: A MUSIC HALL ARTISTE sits inside a cage, suspended in the air, in the pose of "The Thinker". As the play begins "The Thinker" suddenly has an idea, does something to the lock and opens the cage door thereby freeing himself/herself as the cage is lowered. As if this were a remarkable trick the ARTISTE gestures to signal applause. Lights out on the gesture.

Music or sounds of a busy quay side as the lights come up on ANNE inside the cage. The cage door is locked. ANNE is about sixteen years old, but for the past fourteen has been reared by chimpanzees in the wild. ANNE acts like a chimpanzee. She is "naked" and filthy, morose and unhappy. She hoots softly.

> *ANNE'S grandmother, LADY VALERIE BRECK-*
> *NOR, and her companion, ELIZABETH GOOD-*
> *WITHY, enter with a rough looking, armed hunter.*
> *VALERIE is a forceful and striking woman in her late*
> *fifties. ELIZABETH is a stylish, competent woman of*
> *similar age. ANNE'S appearance shocks them both.*)

VALERIE: How could you keep her in this condition?

HUNTER: She's wild, your Ladyship. What was I supposed to do, reason with her?

ELIZABETH:You could have dressed her at least.

> (*The HUNTER clearly finds the suggestion ridicul-*
> *ous.*)

VALERIE: (*to ELIZABETH*) Get her back home. I want the first ship out of Africa. (*to ANNE*) Anne? Little ANNE? It's all right now. We'll soon have you safe.

ELIZABETH:Are you sure it is her?

VALERIE: Give me the photographs.

> (*ELIZABETH takes two photographs from her bag and*
> *hands them to VALERIE.*)

VALERIE: Anne, look: Mummy, Daddy. Look. Anne?

> (*ANNE turns away from the photographs.*)

ELIZABETH:Nothing.

VALERIE: Fourteen years. You expect too much.

HUNTER: We found her near the lake where your son went missing. There have been rumours for years about a white chimpanzee, but... well... I never thought.... She must be about the right age. We found her living with them.

VALERIE: Anne?

> (*ANNE grunts aggressively at VALERIE.*)

HUNTER: I wouldn't go too close, she's got a nasty bite.

ELIZABETH:Valerie, careful.

VALERIE: (*sings*) Rock-a-bye baby on the tree top, when the wind blows the cradle will rock, when the bough breaks the cradle will fall...

> (*ANNE is drawn to VALERIE. She reaches out her hand through the bars and touches VALERIE'S mouth. VALERIE stops singing.*)

VALERIE: Let her out of here now, let her out.

HUNTER: What, here?

VALERIE: Let her out, I said.

HUNTER: She's already injured two of my men.

VALERIE: Give me the key.

HUNTER: I sell what I catch.

VALERIE: This is my granddaughter!

HUNTER: A circus would pay a fortune for her.

VALERIE: (*shouting*) Give me the key now! I said, give it to me!

> (*ANNE reacts badly to the argument and attacks her cage. VALERIE and ELIZABETH are horrified. The HUNTER cocks his rifle. VALERIE stands between them.*)

VALERIE: No!

> (*ANNE waits aggressively for their next move.*)

HUNTER: See what I mean? Now, if you want her, you pay for her, your Ladyship.

ELIZABETH:Perhaps we could go to your office.

> (*VALERIE exits escorted by ELIZABETH. The HUNTER turns to ANNE. Amused, he makes a chimp sound to goad her.*)

SCENE TWO

(*The cage is hoisted into the air as sounds of a quay side and music indicate the journey from Africa. ANNE is bewildered. The set transforms to a stately home in the Welsh borders. As the cage is lowered a tarpaulin is thrown over it, to conceal ANNE.*

Lights up on AUGUSTA and her children, SOPHIE and TIMOTHY. They are inside the Brecknor stately home. AUGUSTA is LADY VALERIE'S niece. She is rather silly and selfish. SOPHIE is 16 and spoilt. TIMOTHY, 18, is rather smug. The family became destitute when AUGUSTA'S husband died. VALERIE took them in and has tried to rear TIMOTHY to take over the estate upon her death. JACQUELINE, a maid, stands subserviently by AUGUSTA. They apply the finishing touches to their costumes. JENKINS, the Head Gardener, and his son, DEWEY, 19, stand in the shadows outside the house, observing the cage. JENKINS has a hoe.)

AUGUSTA: We must look our best.

SOPHIE: Nothing is too good for Great Aunt Valerie. (*sarcastically*)

AUGUSTA: Do try to be charming, Timothy, if only to compensate for your sister's complete lack of it.

TIMOTHY: (*bored*) Yes, Mother.

SOPHIE: Why did they have to go and find Anne? Everyone thought she was dead. Now she's going to inherit and we become poor relations.

AUGUSTA: All the more reason to cultivate charm, child. If Timothy were to marry Anne, our future would be secure once again.

SOPHIE: Let's hope she's pretty.

TIMOTHY: Her appearance hardly matters, Sophie. I have a

duty to my family to find her radiant.

AUGUSTA: Now, how will you greet Anne?

TIMOTHY: May I say how relieved and delighted we are to have you home again, cousin Anne?

AUGUSTA: There you see, Sophie, charm. (*to JACQUELINE*) Is Lady Anne's room prepared?

JACQ: Yes, Ma'am. They should be here any minute, Ma'am. A crate has arrived already. Isn't it exciting?

(*They give her a look, then go to inspect the crate. Lights up on the exterior of the house. The crate smells badly.*)

AUGUSTA: What is it?

JENKINS: The carter wouldn't say, Ma'am, flew off in a terrible hurry.

(*ANNE makes chimp noises softly. They become intrigued by the cage and investigate it.*)

JENKINS: I think there's something in there.

TIMOTHY: Oh, really.

AUGUSTA: What has she brought home this time?

JENKINS: Begging your pardon, Ma'am, the carter gave strict instructions not to remove the tarpaulin.

DEWEY: That's right, Ma'am, Lady Valerie ordered....

AUGUSTA: Jenkins, you and your son remove the tarpaulin.

(*DEWEY and JENKINS do so against their better judgment. They cannot believe their eyes. JACQUELINE faints. They all ignore her.*)

SOPHIE: It's a person.

AUGUSTA: It can't be... this can't be...?

DEWEY: I said it smelt like....

JENKINS: Never mind that now, Dewey.

TIMOTHY: May I say how relieved and delighted we are to have you home, cousin Anne?

SOPHIE: Timothy!

AUGUSTA: This must be a mistake.

TIMOTHY: Well, it's alive which is more than can be said for Aunt Valerie's usual trophies, and far more interesting.

AUGUSTA: Look away, Timothy.

JENKINS: Yes, Dewey, look away.

AUGUSTA: And you, Jenkins! This may yet turn out to be the next Lady Brecknor.

(*The men turn their backs.*)

SOPHIE: Don't be ridiculous, mother, this is an animal! Unless, perhaps, a servant's child was lost in the jungle as well.

(*SOPHIE gets a hoe from JENKINS and begins prodding ANNE with it.*)

TIMOTHY: Perhaps she's gone mad? Fourteen years in the jungle, she's gone mad.

AUGUSTA: If she's mad she can't inherit.

TIMOTHY: Then I'm in the clear.

SOPHIE: Ooh, look, she's soiled herself.

TIMOTHY: You see?

AUGUSTA: She can be potty trained. You were.

TIMOTHY: It is hardly a duty one expects a husband to fulfil. Does she look like a Brecknor?

AUGUSTA: Try to get it to show its face.

(*SOPHIE uses the hoe to raise ANNE'S face.*)

SOPHIE: Oh, she doesn't like that!

(ANNE reacts aggressively to the hoe. The men turn to look.)

TIMOTHY: There is a resemblance to Valerie's old gun dog. Let me have a try.

(TIMOTHY grabs the hoe, but SOPHIE won't let go.)

SOPHIE: No, it was my idea.

AUGUSTA: Don't squabble! Sophie, let Timothy have his turn.

TIMOTHY: Sophie, it's my turn!

JENKINS: Leave the creature alone!

(JENKINS pushes TIMOTHY aside, grabs the hoe from SOPHIE and throws it to the ground in a fury.)

DEWEY: Dad!

JENKINS: Can't you see it's terrified! Have some pity, for God's sake!

AUGUSTA: How dare you talk to my daughter like that?

SOPHIE: He hurt me.

TIMOTHY: *(fearful of JENKINS)* He deserves a good thrashing.

AUGUSTA: Just who do you think you are, Jenkins?

DEWEY: He didn't mean no harm, Ma'am.

TIMOTHY: Leave this to me, mother.

AUGUSTA: Oh, do shut up, Timothy. How dare you lay your hands on my daughter?

JENKINS: *(realising that he has over-reached his status)* The creature's afraid.

(Pause as they realise JENKINS is fearful.)

SOPHIE: Pick that hoe up, Jenkins. Pick it up and hand it to me.

(A tense silence as JENKINS deliberates. He "climbs

down" and presents it to SOPHIE. SOPHIE and TIMOTHY smugly resume torturing ANNE.)

AUGUSTA: Now pack your things and be off the estate within the hour.

(*VALERIE and ELIZABETH enter.*)

VALERIE: What is going on here?

SOPHIE: Aunt Valerie, thank goodness. You would not believe this man's impertinence.

(*VALERIE goes to the cage and looks at ANNE. She sees her in a worse state than ever.*)

AUGUSTA: Jenkins assaulted us with the hoe. He tore it from poor Sophie's grasp.

VALERIE: I see.

AUGUSTA: I have, of course, dismissed him.

JENKINS: If you'll excuse me.

(*JENKINS makes to leave.*)

VALERIE: Stay where you are!

(*A pause as they wait to see what VALERIE will do.*)

VALERIE: This is my granddaughter, Anne. She needs complete peace. Do you understand?

(*VALERIE turns on SOPHIE who hands her the hoe.*)

VALERIE: Tell me, Sophie dear, what is this sudden and violent urge to garden?

SOPHIE: I wasn't gardening.

VALERIE: Perhaps you have discovered a better use for a hoe?

SOPHIE: (*on the verge of tears*) I only wanted to see its face.

(*VALERIE turns SOPHIE'S face with the hoe.*)

VALERIE: How remarkably inventive.

(*VALERIE forces SOPHIE'S head back.*)

ELIZABETH:(*intervening*) Valerie.

VALERIE: Get your offspring into the house, Augusta.

(*AUGUSTA'S family exit hurriedly.*)

ELIZABETH:I'm not sure that was wholly necessary.

VALERIE: Please see to the luggage, Elizabeth.

(*ELIZABETH exits.*)

VALERIE: Jenkins, long service does not give you the right to correct your betters, am I clear? It is hardly a good example to set your son.

JENKINS: I sought to protect the girl, Lady Brecknor.

VALERIE: I want it to be understood by everyone on the estate that my granddaughter's presence is to remain a secret. Anyone betraying my wishes will reap the consequences for the rest of their lives, I promise you. I trust you to help me in this.

JENKINS: I'm sure, Ma'am, that there is not one of us who will feel anything but compassion. Isn't that right, Dewey?

DEWEY: That's right, Ma'am.

(*VALERIE turns her back on the men.*)

JENKINS: And the other lads will understand that, won't they, Dewey? I won't need to impress it upon their persons, will I?

(*JENKINS whilst speaking calmly holds up his fist to DEWEY.*)

DEWEY: No, Dad, I think they'll get the message.

VALERIE: I am reassured. Thank you, gentlemen.

JENKINS: Get on with your work, Dewey.

DEWEY: Sir. Good to have you home again, Lady Valerie.

	Some of us thought you'd peg it out in the jungle.
VALERIE:	(*amused*) Thank you, Dewey.
JENKINS:	(*embarrassed*) On your way, Dewey.
DEWEY:	Sir.

(*DEWEY exits.*)

VALERIE:	He meant well. (*Her attention turns to ANNE.*) Little by little she is fading.
JENKINS:	Pardon me saying, but keep any animal behind bars, forced to soil its own nest, and it will soon sicken.
VALERIE:	She won't eat.
JENKINS:	Doesn't look to me like she wants to live. This is a sickness of the soul.
VALERIE:	Perhaps I should have let her go? Perhaps I was too late? She was better off where she was?
JENKINS:	Who knows what cruelties you have spared her?
VALERIE:	Or what cruelties we shall inflict upon her.
JENKINS:	Have you the key?

(*VALERIE hands JENKINS the key. He unlocks the cage and opens the door. Lights change as a girl in a playpen is carried past ANNE. This is a memory and we are seeing it. ANNE leaves her cage and sits downstage as JENKINS and VALERIE exit.*

The original production had a three-year-old girl playing young ANNE. If this is not possible, then ANNE should get into the playpen as RUTH sings to her. She is transferring from one cage to another.)

SCENE THREE

(Lights change to the jungle. GEOFFREY BRECK-NOR, VALERIE'S son, sits at a camp table studying a leaf and a reference book. RUTH, his wife, sings 'Rock-a-bye Baby' to little ANNE.)

GEOFFREY: Ruth, take a look at this.

(RUTH goes across to him.)

RUTH: That's interesting. Strange colouring.

GEOFFREY: I can't find any reference to it anywhere.

RUTH: How marvellous. *(to ANNE)* See what a clever Daddy you've got?

(RUTH crosses to ANNE with the leaf. GEOFFREY follows.)

GEOFFREY: If it is undiscovered I could name it after Anne.

RUTH: Oh, yes.

GEOFFREY: Look at this, young lady. What do you think, eh?

RUTH: What will you call it?

GEOFFREY: Brecknoranthus.

RUTH: Lovely.

GEOFFREY: I need to get a root sample.

(He begins to get a trowel and a shoulder bag.)

RUTH: Not now, surely? I've told the servants to serve dinner in half an hour. I thought perhaps we could have a drink, play with Anne.

GEOFFREY: I'd love to, of course. Look, you pour the drinks, I'll be back by the time you've finished.

RUTH: Well, don't get all muddy again.

GEOFFREY: All right, I promise.

99

(*They kiss.*)

RUTH: Silly boy. Well? Go on, then.

(*GEOFFREY exits happily whilst RUTH goes into their tent.*

The CHIMPS, led by ADAM, slowly emerge, confused by the changes to their range. They investigate baby ANNE and the curious objects around them. BEN arrives and the atmosphere changes. BEN defers to ADAM. RUTH hears their calls and comes out. She attempts to shoo them away which enrages and scares them. RUTH runs into the tent and reemerges with a rifle. ALICE, the alpha female is by baby ANNE, as is BEN. RUTH shoots and kills ALICE'S child. ADAM attacks RUTH and kills her.

GEOFFREY: (*offstage*) Ruth!

(*Spooked, the CHIMPS leave the camp. ALICE is uncertain and has to leave the body of her child behind.*

GEOFFREY, having heard the gunshot, runs into camp to find the dead body of his wife. BEN suddenly jumps down. GEOFFREY picks up the rifle but it is empty. He swings it at BEN instead. To his amazement BEN picks up a fallen section of a branch. The two animals scream and yell at each other. BEN clubs GEOFFREY to death.

ADAM leads the other CHIMPS back on. ALICE is distraught and tries to get her dead baby to move. The other chimps watch her grief. ALICE goes to baby ANNE and lifts her out of the playpen. [If a child is not used then ANNE symbolically gives her younger self to ALICE who mimes carrying her off.] ALICE is defended by BRUNO and BESSIE, two of her older children. ALICE takes the baby off stage. ADAM signals for the colony to follow them. BEN remains gloating over the dead bodies, then moves downstage to where ANNE is remembering this scene. She becomes afraid of him. He threatens her before exiting.

TARZANNE

The bodies of a dead woman, man and baby lie on stage.)

SCENE FOUR

(*Night. Sounds of ANNE screeching and the shouts and excited cries of VALERIE, AUGUSTA and ELIZABETH. SOPHIE enters the stage, curious as to the reason for the noise. TIMOTHY enters separately.*)

SOPHIE: What on earth are they doing?

TIMOTHY: Trying to get the creature into a bath, apparently.

(*JACQUELINE, carrying towels, miserably crosses the stage.*)

TIMOTHY: How's it going, Jacqueline?

(*She exits with a groan.*)

TIMOTHY: Do get along and help, Sophie.

SOPHIE: Timothy, if you marry that creature I shall never forgive you.

TIMOTHY: Believe me, Sophie, that day shall never come to pass. I have a little plan already up my sleeve.

VALERIE: (*offstage*) Jacqueline, mind out!

(*JACQUELINE screams.*)

VALERIE: Stupid girl. Augusta, catch her!

(*AUGUSTA screams.*)

ELIZABETH: For goodness' sake, Augusta. Now, where's she gone?

(*ANNE enters stage right and scurries past SOPHIE and TIMOTHY. ANNE is in an indignant mood. She exits stage left. VALERIE enters stage right with*

101

> *ELIZABETH. They hold bath towels. VALERIE is enjoying herself. ELIZABETH is not.*)

SOPHIE: Where were you? I had her right here.

VALERIE: Damn! Which way did she go?

TIMOTHY: (*lying*) That way.

> (*AUGUSTA enters, exhausted.*)

VALERIE: Do keep up, Augusta.

> (*AUGUSTA whines.*)

ELIZABETH:Shouldn't we get a net or something?

VALERIE: She's too quick for us. Marvellous, isn't she? First sign of life since we found her. Geoffrey was the same, always hid at bath time.

ELIZABETH:Really.

VALERIE: Let's split up.

AUGUSTA: But what if I find her?

ELIZABETH:Then hang on to her, Augusta!

SOPHIE: Try using charm, mother.

VALERIE: Jacqueline, do hurry up.

> (*VALERIE exits in one direction.*)

ELIZABETH:Sophie, we expect you to help.

SOPHIE: Why certainly, Elizabeth. I shall be right behind you.

> (*ELIZABETH exits in another direction, as does AUGUSTA. SOPHIE stays put. JACQUELINE slops across stage from stage left to stage right.*)

TIMOTHY: Good girl, Jacqueline. That's the spirit.

> (*JACQUELINE groans.*)

SOPHIE: So what's your plan? Timmy, tell me.

(AUGUSTA enters, whingeing.)

AUGUSTA: Sophie! You are supposed to be helping.

SOPHIE: I am mother, in my own way.

TIMOTHY: Have you managed to propose on my behalf yet, mother, or haven't you found quite the right note to scream at yet?

(AUGUSTA goes to exit stage left and screams as ANNE enters. ANNE menacingly stalks AUGUSTA.)

AUGUSTA: Sophie! Timothy, help me! Help me, I said!

(They do nothing, but watch with glee.)

AUGUSTA: Help me! Please.

(ANNE jumps onto AUGUSTA knocking her to the ground and sits on her. VALERIE and ELIZABETH enter.)

VALERIE: Well done, Augusta. Don't move.

(The WOMEN close in on ANNE, surrounding her with bath towels.)

VALERIE: Come on now, Anne. Bath time. Be good.

(AUGUSTA tries to get away and ANNE slips past the WOMEN.)

VALERIE: After her!

(VALERIE and ELIZABETH exit, leaving AUGUSTA on her knees.)

AUGUSTA: I shall not forget this, Timothy!

TIMOTHY: Do hurry up, mother, my fianceé is about to escape to the outside world.

(AUGUSTA exits in a hurry.)

SOPHIE: Timmy, what is your plan?

(TIMOTHY exits, smiling.)

SOPHIE: Timmy, tell me!

(*SOPHIE exits after TIMOTHY.*)

SCENE FIVE

(*Lights up on the greenhouse at night. JENKINS is working outside. ANNE bolts on stage, sees JENKINS, then sneaks into the greenhouse behind his back. ANNE loves the greenhouse's smells, plants and warmth. JENKINS enters and disturbs her. They are equally shocked by each other. JENKINS is embarrassed by her nakedness. ANNE is confused by his body language.*)

JENKINS: Erm... does your grandmother know you're here? Eh? Look, you'd better put something on.

(*JENKINS holds out a sack. ANNE assumes it to be another towel and growls fiercely at him. He puts the sack down.*)

JENKINS: All right! All right! I don't know about this... glasshouse and everything.

(*JENKINS goes to the greenhouse door and shouts out.*)

JENKINS: Help!

(*ANNE becomes agitated. JENKINS tries to shout quietly.*)

JENKINS: Help.

(*ANNE reacts again.*)

JENKINS: Sorry, sorry, please don't break anything. Please.

(*ANNE sits on the workbench. She seems to be claiming the greenhouse as her own and sits imperiously.*)

JENKINS: Oi! This is my greenhouse, don't you go getting any ideas. Remind you of home, does it?

(JENKINS goes towards her and she jumps down and hides.)

JENKINS: Where you hiding?

(ANNE pokes her head out.)

JENKINS: Boo!

(ANNE is amazed. Perhaps she remembers this game.)

ANNE: Ooh!

JENKINS: No, boo! Boo!

(ANNE hides again. JENKINS sneaks about. ANNE appears.)

ANNE: Ooh!

JENKINS: Boo!

(JENKINS gets an apple.)

JENKINS: Here, want an apple?

(She won't take it from his hand.)

JENKINS: All right, then.

(He leaves it for her on the workbench. She uses a tool to reach for it.)

JENKINS: *(amused)* Tools.

(ANNE eats the apple.)

JENKINS: Apple. Apple. You like it?

(ANNE moves towards him, intent upon working out what he is. For example, is that skin he is wearing or is there something like her own body underneath? JENKINS is glued to the spot, frightened to move.)

JENKINS: Now stay calm, Miss Anne. No sudden movements, all right?

(*ANNE climbs onto the bench, grabs JENKINS and wraps a leg over his shoulder to hold him still whilst she investigates. ANNE has the apple in her mouth. She reaches down inside his shirt to feel him. VALERIE appears, followed by ELIZABETH.*)

VALERIE: Good man, Jenkins.

JENKINS: Yes, Ma'am.

ELIZABETH:Jenkins, what are you...?

VALERIE: Ssh!

ELIZABETH:What is this exactly, Jenkins, the Garden of Eden?

(*VALERIE laughs.*)

JENKINS: It's her fault. I couldn't help it, Ma'am.

ELIZABETH:Yes. Well, no doubt that's what Adam said as well.

VALERIE: Let's grab her now.

JENKINS: No, please, Ma'am, not in my greenhouse.

VALERIE: Get her!

(*They pounce. JENKINS lifts ANNE in order to save his greenhouse. ANNE bites him.*)

VALERIE: Get her into the house, Jenkins.

JENKINS: She bit me, the little demon! She bit me!

SCENE SIX

(*JENKINS carries ANNE across the stage. VALERIE, ELIZABETH and JACQUELINE are then seen pouring water over ANNE'S hair. JENKINS returns to the greenhouse where he remains throughout the scene.*)

(A clap of thunder and the stage is transformed to the jungle.)

ELIZABETH:She's frightened.

VALERIE: Perhaps she is remembering something.

(BEN appears and displays violently to ANNE. ADAM enters and sees BEN off. ALICE enters and ANNE wants to go to her for comfort.)

VALERIE: Let her go. See what she does.

(ANNE joins ALICE, her chimp mother. Other chimps enter. Lights fade on VALERIE and ELIZABETH. The chimps are uneasy in this thunderstorm. ANNE gets a large leaf to keep the rain off herself. ALICE is intrigued and tries to touch it. ANNE grunts for her to leave it alone. ALICE observes ANNE then puts her arms over her head in an imitation of shelter. ALICE is very pleased with herself. ANNE thinks she is stupid. Another chimp tries to take the leaf. ALICE and ANNE grunt to tell her to go. A third chimp nestles in beside ANNE and tries to get under the leaf. After three attempts, ANNE grunts and she too goes. ADAM has been watching this and goes to ANNE. He sits looking at the leaf, then up at the rain. He looks sorry for himself. ANNE relents to the higher status of ADAM and very grumpily puts the leaf on ADAM'S head and holds it there for him. ADAM is satisfied. ALICE, seeing her daughter without protection puts one of her hands on ANNE'S head. BEN moves in closely and the chimps react to his dangerous presence. BEN defers to ADAM and ALICE but attacks ANNE. ALICE tries to fend him off, but it is only when ADAM intervenes that BEN runs away. ANNE is grateful and cuddles into ADAM.

JENKINS appears as lights come up on the greenhouse.)

JENKINS: Miss Anne, you out here again? You'll catch your death, child.

(ANNE looks from JENKINS to ADAM. ADAM gets up to leave. The other chimps exit. ANNE says goodbye to ADAM, her protector, and goes to JENKINS, her new protector, in the greenhouse. JENKINS begins to dry her hair.)

SCENE SEVEN

(Lights up on JENKINS and ANNE as they also come up on ELIZABETH who brushes VALERIE'S hair. VALERIE holds a pillow.)

ELIZABETH:I confess to being amazed. How can you let this continue? A naked girl and a gardener.

VALERIE: He is the only one who can get her to eat.

ELIZABETH:If this ever gets to the newspapers, you will probably be arrested for immorality.

VALERIE: And if she died, what would they arrest me for? Ow!

ELIZABETH:Sorry. Valerie, you are hardly in your prime.

VALERIE: Thank you.

ELIZABETH:You cannot run the estate, the mills, the finances, and look after Anne. The damage done to her is so profound. She should be somewhere secure.

VALERIE: An asylum? Why have I searched for fourteen years? To send her to a madhouse?

ELIZABETH:We have found her too late.

VALERIE: Give her time. She is trying to make sense of what is happening to her.

ELIZABETH:Have you lost your common sense as well as your morals? If this were someone else you would condemn them.

VALERIE: But this is me and that is my granddaughter and I need her.

ELIZABETH:Love makes fools of us all, doesn't it?

SCENE EIGHT

(*NEWSPAPER SELLERS shout: "Read all about it", "Heiress found in jungle", "Chimpanzee girl is heir to fortune", "Chimp girl eightieth in line to the throne".*

TIMOTHY walks across the stage with a newspaper. He looks very pleased with himself. The MUSIC HALL ARTISTE pays him handsomely then turns to the audience and begins to sing.)

I met a girl the other day
As regal as could be.
She rode within a carriage grand in all her finery.
I strutted up and tipped me cap
Then unashamedly
My true love scratched her armpit
And grunted down to me.

Ooh! Ooh! Ah-ah-ah!
My love's a chimpanzee!
She likes the odd banana
and swinging in the trees
Ooh! Ooh! Ah-ah-ah!
My love's a chimpanzee
She tipped me the wink
But I had to think
What price nobility?

Now we live in a tree house
Just south of Oswestry.

It's not as grand as I had planned
And Mum won't visit me.

Though we're the Duke and Duchess
Of all that we can see,
If I'd had a mind I should have declined
To join this family's tree.

(*The MUSIC HALL ARTISTE is joined by another
ARTISTE who is dressed in a hairy chimp suit and
mask. The "chimp" wears a skirt and a hat with a
comical flower on it. They dance.*)

Ooh! Ooh! Ah-ah-ah!
I've maried a chimpanzee
I eat the odd banana
But miss me cup of tea.
Ooh! Ooh! Ah-ah-ah!
I've married a chimpanzee
And despite what you say
I swing today
In high society.

Whilst others may jest and mock us,
At least I've come to see
That my true love's not the only chimp
In the aristocracy.

(*Lights up on VALERIE and ELIZABETH who stand
in VALERIE'S study. They observe the singer.*)

Altogether now!

Ooh! Ooh! Ah-ah-ah!
My love's a chimpanzee,
Though I had in mind
A different kind of high society.
Ooh! Ooh! Ah-ah-ah!

I've married a chimpanzee,
Though her manners ain't grand
I'm a happy man
In high society!

(*The song turns ominious at the end. Lights down on the music hall.*)

SCENE NINE

(*VALERIE sits and looks at business documents. ELIZABETH stands and lights change to show an interior study. ELIZABETH signals for JACQUE-LINE to show AUGUSTA, SOPHIE and TIMOTHY in. VALERIE passes ELIZABETH a document. They act as if they had not noticed the arrival of AUG-USTA'S family. ELIZABETH looks up from the papers.*)

ELIZABETH:Lady Valerie was wondering if you had read the newspapers today?

AUGUSTA: Yes, indeed.

SOPHIE: It was humiliating.

AUGUSTA: Poor Valerie, did you see the cartoon? I thought that quite unnecessary.

(*VALERIE gives AUGUSTA a withering look.*)

ELIZABETH:Lady Valerie has shares in the newspaper, Timothy. The editor was only too pleased to disclose the source of the story. It seems Timothy was paid twenty pounds for it by a journalist in a public house in Farringdon.

TIMOTHY: This is nonsense.

AUGUSTA: You went to a public house?

ELIZABETH: Augusta.

SOPHIE: Was that your great plan? Oh, brilliant! Most people have a mad granny locked in the attic and manage to keep it a secret. But us, we have a monkey woman in a greenhouse and you let everyone know.

VALERIE: Sophie, shut up. Jacqueline, are Master Timothy's bags packed?

JACQUELINE: Yes, Ma'am and the carriage is waiting.

TIMOTHY: What carriage?

VALERIE: Whilst you were stuffing your faces with my bacon I have enlisted Timothy in the army as a common foot soldier. There I hope you shall learn the importance of loyalty, honour and trust.

TIMOTHY: A foot soldier?

AUGUSTA: I'm not sure he'd be terribly good at it, Valerie.

TIMOTHY: I shan't go!

ELIZABETH: In that instance your mother and sister shall leave the house with you. The carriage will take you to the end of the drive. The rest is up to you.

SOPHIE: This isn't fair.

VALERIE: He has destroyed all chance that Anne might grow in peace, turned her into a freak for idle curiosity! Why should you have peace? Now you shall learn what it means to survive. Get out.

SOPHIE: Don't let them do this, Mama.

AUGUSTA: Wait. Timothy, you must go, make amends.

TIMOTHY: You would send me to my death?

AUGUSTA: You fool. Would you send us to ours for twenty pounds?

ELIZABETH:I take it a decision has been reached?

> (*TIMOTHY exits. VALERIE looks at AUGUSTA who turns and leaves with SOPHIE. Once they are gone ELIZABETH and VALERIE relax. VALERIE appears very weak.*)

VALERIE: Thank you.

> (*ELIZABETH goes to her side. VALERIE rests her head on ELIZABETH and is comforted by her.*)

VALERIE: From now on, no-one leaves the estate.

SCENE TEN

> (*Lights up on the greenhouse at night. JENKINS pots a banana plant. ANNE examines herself in a mirror.*)

JENKINS: Mirror. Mirror. Anne. Anne.

> (*JENKINS gets an encyclopaedia and opens it at a marked page.*)

JENKINS: Encyclo... no, never mind that. Look here, chimpanzee.

> (*ANNE looks at the drawing of a chimpanzee in the book and is amazed.*)

JENKINS: Now, look again. (*He holds up the mirror.*) Anne. Anne. (*then points at the book*) Chimpanzee.

> (*VALERIE has approached the greenhouse. She watches.*)

VALERIE: Jenkins.

JENKINS: (*awkwardly*) Lady Valerie. Erm... cold night tonight.

> (*ANNE takes the mirror and looks at herself.*)

VALERIE: It's warm in there, isn't it?

JENKINS: Yes.

VALERIE: Then invite me in, man.

JENKINS: You're welcome.

(*JENKINS gets her a rough wooden stool to sit on.*)

VALERIE: What's that?

(*She refers to the banana plant.*)

JENKINS: Well... I thought I'd have a go at growing bananas.

VALERIE: Preposterous man.... Is she well?

JENKINS: She's eaten. Lost in thought, she is.

VALERIE: She likes you. (*he shrugs*) Why? Sit down, man. I can't stand you lumbering over me.

(*JENKINS sits down.*)

VALERIE: Tell me.

JENKINS: She's an animal... if you'll excuse the presumption. We all need physical loving. I mean, children need it to grow.

VALERIE: Perhaps it's not only children?

JENKINS: Ah, well. Would her Ladyship like a tot of whisky? Keep you warm.

(*VALERIE accepts his offer and he gets up to pour some whisky into two rough cups as VALERIE speaks.*)

VALERIE: I suppose I must be a very difficult person to touch. People want me to be strong, you see. They hang on to the belief that I at least know what is happening. I've forgotten how to touch. Certainly since my husband...

(*JENKINS hands her the drink.*)

VALERIE: You must miss your wife terribly.

JENKINS: Aye, Ma'am.

(Two people from different classes share bereavement. VALERIE holds out her cup and JENKINS raises his to VALERIE'S. They drink.)

VALERIE: My parents never held me, certainly.

JENKINS: Ah, well now, I've been reading. See, likelihood is, Anne's mother would have carried her on her back.

VALERIE: You mean the chimpanzees?

JENKINS: Sorry, yes. I reckon your Miss Anne don't know who she is nor where she is. She needs to decide.

VALERIE: But if she does accept us, Jenkins, I fear the world will never accept her, not now everybody knows about her condition.

JENKINS: Well, I can't say about that, but I do know this. She won't choose us if we don't love her, will she?

(They look at ANNE studying herself in the mirror as ELIZABETH enters.)

ELIZABETH:Valerie!

VALERIE: Ssh! Look at Anne.

ELIZABETH:What are you doing out here? You'll catch your death.

(ANNE looks up at ELIZABETH.)

VALERIE: Damn, you disturbed her.

(ANNE takes the mirror across to ELIZABETH, looks into it, then at ELIZABETH. ANNE reaches to touch ELIZABETH'S face.)

JENKINS: It's as if she's working something out.

ELIZABETH:How can that be? You are deluding yourselves and it is very sad to see.

115

(*ANNE takes the mirror away and looks at it again, remembering an earlier incident in the jungle.*)

SCENE ELEVEN

(*Lights come up on the jungle and ANNE enters it. She meets ALICE and they are affectionate. The human characters remain on stage. Their attention is fixed upon ANNE. A mother and child elephant enter. ANNE hides and observes them as they drink from a watering hole. The baby spots ANNE and is curious.*)

ANNE: Mm... Mm... Mm....

(*Chimps are heard approaching and the elephant shepherds her baby away. ADAM enters first and greets ANNE. The chimps enter and are curious about the objects they find in the wrecked camp. ANNE finds her mother's mirror and is confused by it. BEN enters and attacks ANNE. When ADAM intervenes BEN decides to fight him. BEN uses a stick to beat ADAM. ADAM scurries away, injured. Now BEN is the alpha male. The other chimps go one by one to defer to him. Finally it is ALICE'S turn. ALICE then tells ANNE to follow suit. ANNE does not want to but ALICE insists. As ANNE approaches BEN he turns on her. ALICE tries to save her but BEN shoos the other chimps away forcing them to abandon ANNE. BEN drives ALICE away. ANNE is between ALICE and VALERIE when VALERIE speaks.*)

VALERIE: Anne, little Anne? I'm going now.

(*ALICE calls to ANNE. ANNE looks from VALERIE to ALICE as if deciding which to choose. ANNE looks once more into the mirror and bids ALICE farewell. ANNE looks at VALERIE.*)

TARZANNE

ANNE: Mumm... mummy... mummy.

(The humans are amazed. ANNE climbs onto VALERIE'S lap. VALERIE, surprised and awkward, looks at JENKINS, then folds her arms around ANNE.)

VALERIE: There now, there now... we're all right, we're going to be all right.

SCENE TWELVE

(A dance sequence in which AUGUSTA, SOPHIE, VALERIE and ELIZABETH dress and groom ANNE. ANNE wears a simple dress in which she remains free to move. She comes to stand upright, but her knees remain bent and turned out. The individual characters' attitudes to ANNE are present in the dance. At the end of the dance, VALERIE and ELIZABETH sit happily as in the garden. Elsewhere, AUGUSTA and SOPHIE do likewise. It is a sunny day. ANNE goes to the greenhouse where JENKINS and DEWEY are working.)

SCENE THIRTEEN

(The women are in good spirits.)

VALERIE: She is learning.

ELIZABETH:Yes, to be a gardener.

VALERIE: *(amused)* Learning gets harder as we get older. Some of us stop altogether.

117

ELIZABETH:I've admitted I was wrong, but if Anne is to progress she needs a hard task master. A teacher who is not emotionally attached to her.

SCENE FOURTEEN

(*The greenhouse. ANNE disturbs JENKINS and demands something by using a rhythmic grunt and by walking her fingers across the work bench. He knows what she wants. She has probably asked for it twenty times today. JENKINS stops work and tries to be enthusiastic. He does a routine of gestures as he speaks. ANNE tries to copy the rhythm and gestures. DEWEY is amused.*)

JENKINS: There was a little man
Who had a little gun,
And up the chimney he did run,
With a big top hat,
And a belly full of fat,
And a pancake tied to his

ANNE: Bum, bum, bum!

(*JENKINS pinches ANNE'S cheek affectionately.*)

JENKINS: Good girl, Anne. Good girl!

(*ANNE and JENKINS clap. DEWEY looks dryly at his father.*)

SCENE FIFTEEN

VALERIE: All right, Elizabeth, place an advertisement in the *Times*.

ELIZABETH:At last.

VALERIE: Lady Anne Brecknor's Coming Out Ball will be held on her birthday, three years hence.

ELIZABETH: A Coming Out Ball!

SCENE SIXTEEN

(*Lights up on SOPHIE and AUGUSTA. AUGUSTA sits in a deck chair, eyes closed.*)

SOPHIE: Three years? No mention of me?

AUGUSTA: No mention, whatsoever.

SOPHIE: I am clothed, fed and housed, yet I am a prisoner here.

AUGUSTA: As I am, my dear, as I am. Personally, I find sleep a great consoler.

(*SOPHIE is frustrated and furious.*)

SCENE SEVENTEEN

(*Lights up on the greenhouse. DEWEY is working but becoming more interested in ANNE. ANNE has progressed. JENKINS gives ANNE an apple.*)

ANNE: Mine? Mine apple?

JENKINS: Yes, yours.

ANNE: No, not yours, mine.

JENKINS: That's what I was....

(*JENKINS takes another apple.*)

119

ANNE: That yours.

JENKINS: Then which one is mine?

ANNE: (*of her own apple*) This mine.

JENKINS: I see. (*of his apple*) So this is yours?

(*ANNE then takes JENKINS' apple as well. She pinches his cheek as she speaks.*)

ANNE: That right, Jenkins, good girl, good girl. You not got apple?

DEWEY: There's not much needs teaching you, is there?

SCENE EIGHTEEN

(*Lights up on VALERIE and ELIZABETH. VALERIE is wrapped in a blanket. They walk in the gardens.*)

ELIZABETH: Each bout of malaria leaves you weaker.

VALERIE: I sometimes think that it is the price for my obsession.

ELIZABETH: You should be having this time in your life to yourself. You've earned it. We should be in Italy where you can convalesce, like in the old days.

VALERIE: That would be selfish.

ELIZABETH: Valerie, you keep us all trapped here so that Anne can be free. Isn't that selfish?

VALERIE: Perhaps.

ELIZABETH: It seems that we are all paying the price of your latest obsession. What if Anne is not ready for her ball?

VALERIE: She loves me. She will not disappoint me.

ELIZABETH:Sometimes loving someone isn't enough.

VALERIE: Anne will not only be ready for her ball, Elizabeth, she will one day run this estate. When I look into her eyes I see myself.

             (*VALERIE exits followed by ELIZABETH.*)

SCENE NINETEEN

             (*JENKINS, ANNE and DEWEY have wooden swords. They are acting out the story of Gwydion from the Mabinogion.*)

DEWEY: But the evil Arianrhod was tricked. "Ah", she said, "The fair-haired boy did it with a skilful hand".

JENKINS: "That he did", said Gwydion. "And now you have named him! Lleu Skilful Hand, he shall be known!"

ANNE: Me be Gwydion now.

JENKINS: (*exasperated*) You just said you wanted to be Lleu Skilful Hand.

ANNE: No, I be Gwydion, you be Arianrhod, Dewey be Lleu.

JENKINS: Who am I now, then?

DEWEY: Arianrhod.

JENKINS: Arianrhod.

ANNE: No! (*better idea*) Dewey be Arianrhod, then Gwydion kiss her.

JENKINS: Gwydion doesn't kiss Arianrhod. They hate each other!

ANNE: Can if he wants to.

DEWEY: Look, I'll be Lleu, he's Gwydion's best friend.

           (*ANNE thinks.*)

ANNE: Yes, Jenkins! Dewey be Lleu!

JENKINS: Begging your pardon, I'm sure.

ANNE: "You name him Lleu Skilful Hand!". Then what happen next?

JENKINS: Then Gwydion changed back to his normal shape.

DEWEY: No, he turned the ship back to kelp first!

JENKINS: No, he didn't. Look, who told you this story?!

DEWEY: You always used to turn the ship back to seaweed first!

ANNE: Not the ship?

JENKINS: Yes, the ship!

ANNE: What, all of it?

DEWEY: Yes, all of it!

ANNE: Oh, I like the ship.

           (*The men groan.*)

DEWEY: Look, you're Gwydion, turn yourself back to your normal shape, and me, cause I'm Lleu. Right. Go on, then.

ANNE: (*makes a strange noise*)

JENKINS: What she doing?

DEWEY: Casting the spell.

JENKINS: Oh.

ANNE: Go on then, Jenkins, see us.

JENKINS: Oh, right. Arianrhod could not believe her eyes. "Gwydion and my son! You have tricked me!"

(*ANNE is delighted.*)

JENKINS: Now, turn the ship back to seaweed.

ANNE: No, cause then Lleu and Gwydion have to swim. They get back on ship.

DEWEY: Just do it.

(*DEWEY climbs aboard the workbench next to ANNE.*)

ANNE: And Gwydion kiss Lleu.

(*ANNE kisses DEWEY. DEWEY is awkward.*)

ANNE: Jenkins? I change my shape. I change from chimp.

JENKINS: Yes, Anne. You're a young woman.

(*DEWEY and JENKINS realise that the days of innocence are numbered, that ANNE is developing "inappropriate" feelings towards DEWEY.*)

ANNE: What... what...?

SCENE TWENTY

(*JENKINS exits. DEWEY leaves ANNE alone. He walks into the garden. ANNE looks up at DEWEY as she pots a rose. As the MUSIC HALL ARTISTE sings a gentle version of the earlier song, DEWEY stops and looks back at ANNE in the greenhouse. They are clearly in love.*)

ARTISTE: Ooh, ooh, ah-ah-ah,
My love's a chimpanzee,
And though she really loves me,
She's aristocracy.

But oh, my little monkey

If you'd groom me hair
I'd swing from a branch,
In a lover's trance
And would not have a care.

(*SOPHIE enters. She is taking a walk in the grounds at dusk. When DEWEY sees her approaching he exits. The action continues as the ARTISTE exits.*)

SCENE TWENTY-ONE

(*SOPHIE watches ANNE tending to a hybrid rose before interrupting her.*)

SOPHIE: So this is what you get up to. (*Pause.*) What are you up to, exactly?

ANNE: A rose. Jenkins and me maked it.

SOPHIE: You mean, you grew it.

ANNE: No, I mean we maked it. This is a new rose, new colours and it flowers two times a year, not one. This is my rose. Me.

SOPHIE: A new rose. I didn't know one could do that.

ANNE: Human beings change shape, make better. One day I go back to jungle make banana this big! (*indicating a huge banana*) Then chimps not go hungry. You want to help?

SOPHIE: No, it's all right.

ANNE: (*pause*) Timothy at war now?

SOPHIE: Yes, three years and not even a letter.

ANNE: Many men killed. Bits hacked off! Blood everywhere! Like chimps they fight for ground to live on.

SOPHIE:	Who on earth told you this?
ANNE:	Dewey, Jenkins.
SOPHIE:	Well, they shouldn't.
ANNE:	It wrong to know things?
SOPHIE:	No, but... it's so unpleasant. You shouldn't be bothered by such things.
ANNE:	I want to know.
SOPHIE:	Why? It's not as if you can change anything.
ANNE:	(*astonished*) Once upon a time man live in caves, don't speak. Now human being speak and tell things. Human being learn and change their shape, see? Chimp never change, chimp always chimp. Maybe you not want to speak, be human?
SOPHIE:	Of course I do. I mean, I am.
ANNE:	Then change shape of war.

(*SOPHIE is surprised by ANNE.*)

SOPHIE:	What will you call your new rose?
ANNE:	Dewey.
SOPHIE:	Oh!
ANNE:	When I give it to him he know I love him for ever as long as the world lives.
SOPHIE:	Anne, have you talked to Valerie about this, or Elizabeth?
ANNE:	Don't worry, I give them next rose I make.
SOPHIE:	No, Anne, you cannot fall in love with Dewey.
ANNE:	Too late. Have to marry him now.
SOPHIE:	No, Anne. They won't let you.
ANNE:	Who said?
SOPHIE:	If you marry it will have to be someone... oh.

	You'll have to marry a Lord, someone with a big house.
ANNE:	We got big house, what I want two for?
SOPHIE:	Oh dear.
ANNE:	You fall in love?
SOPHIE:	Who with? I'm not allowed to meet anybody.
ANNE:	You not fall in love with Dewey. Him mine.
SOPHIE:	I assure you I shall not fall for Dewey.
ANNE:	How does human girl get a mate?
SOPHIE:	A mate?!
ANNE:	Yes. When chimpanzee woman want mate her bottom gets big.
SOPHIE:	Big?
ANNE:	Huge. Then man chimp know she want mate. Easy. Does your bottom get big when you want mate?
SOPHIE:	Certainly not!
ANNE:	Good, I was getting worried. Then, how man know what girl want?
SOPHIE:	One... plays the piano... I don't know.
ANNE:	Ah, poor old Sophie. No man love you. When I chimp, no man chimp love me. Me not understand why.

SCENE TWENTY-TWO

(*Flash back to jungle. This should be played as if ANNE is telling SOPHIE an anecdote. Therefore, SOPHIE can see the chimpanzees.*

ANNE greets ALICE who enters first.

*An elderly female chimp, alone and tired, enters.
ANNE stops playing with ALICE and points out the
new female chimp to SOPHIE. The old female looks
around, relieved to be alone. She sits and rolls on her
back before coming to sit, satisfied that she can relax in
peace. Suddenly her youngest DAUGHER enters. The
old, harrassed MOTHER sighs heavily as the child
begins demanding attention. A SECOND YOUNG
CHIMP enters and squabbles with the child over the
MOTHER. The MOTHER looks forlorn. A THIRD
YOUNG CHIMP enters and joins the squabble,
followed by a FOURTH. The poor MOTHER chimp is
exhausted. She gets up and moves to sit elsewhere. The
YOUNG CHIMPS carry on squabbling until they
notice that the MOTHER has moved. They stop, look,
then chase off to surround her, once more squabbling
for her attention.*

*Some OTHER CHIMPS enter and play before
ADAM enters with BESSIE, a mature female who is in
season. ANNE leaves SOPHIE and enters the
flashback again. ADAM and BESSIE settle down to
mate. ANNE tries to intervene but is brushed aside.
When ANNE tries to get between them the chimps
shoo ANNE away before going off elsewhere to mate in
peace. ANNE is left feeling rejected. ALICE offers out
her hand in comfort but ANNE, like a moody teenager,
rejects her mother's help. ALICE shrugs and sighs.*

ANNE returns to SOPHIE and the present.)

SCENE TWENTY-THREE

(*Back to the greenhouse.*)

ANNE: Me understand now; different species. Now me

	love Dewey, same species.
SOPHIE:	Yes, but....
ANNE:	What?
SOPHIE:	(*amused*) Why do you have to make everything so uncomplicated: Will you tell me more about the chimpanzees, your mother? What was it like? Weren't you frightened?
ANNE:	One chimp hate me.
	(*BEN displays to ANNE. He has been lurking up a tree.*)
ANNE:	'Cause I'm different. Humans put me in cage because I'm different.
SOPHIE:	Yes. Listen, when you first arrived....
ANNE:	I remember.
SOPHIE:	I'm sorry.
	(*DEWEY and JENKINS enter. The are in a foul temper and argue in the garden.*)
JENKINS:	Why didn't you talk to me first?
ANNE:	(*to SOPHIE*) Dewey.
	(*ANNE picks up the rose to give to DEWEY.*)
DEWEY:	Because I knew you'd say no.
JENKINS:	I can't believe that you'd throw all this away for a lousy job in a mill.
DEWEY:	I've got to go.
JENKINS:	Why? It makes no sense. The men in our family grew this place from seed.
DEWEY:	Aye, but Lady Valerie tells you what you can and cannot take from this garden.
JENKINS:	Your mother must be turning in her grave.

DEWEY: Mum would have wanted me to go. I'll get cash, I'll have my own place, my own food, my own life, not yours and not Lady Valerie's.

JENKINS: What are you talking about, boy? She owns the ruddy mills an' all.

DEWEY: I don't expect you to understand, Dad.

JENKINS: At least if the price of wool drops I've still got a roof and food.

DEWEY: The world has changed. I've got choices you never had.

JENKINS: You've always had to do things your own way, haven't you? Well, you go. I'll find another who'll be grateful for all I can teach him. You'd never have made it anyway.

DEWEY: Oh, wouldn't I?

JENKINS: No, you haven't got it in you.

DEWEY: I could have, but nothing is ever good enough for you. Maybe that's why I'm getting out. To get away from you!

            (*ANNE puts down the rose and runs out of the greenhouse and in between the men.*)

ANNE: Stop it!

DEWEY: Anne.

ANNE: You not go.

DEWEY: I've got to.

JENKINS: Excuse us, Miss Anne, this has got nothing to do with you.

DEWEY: I've got to.

ANNE: No, please.

            (*DEWEY exits.*)

ANNE: What you done! What you done, Jenkins!

            (*ANNE strikes JENKINS.*)

SOPHIE: Anne, stop it!

JENKINS: What's got into you, girl?

            (*ANNE stops suddenly. She is in great distress and runs off. SOPHIE follows her. Lights cross fade to VALERIE'S study.*)

SCENE TWENTY-FOUR

(*VALERIE and ELIZABETH interview MRS HARD-WICK, a prim, authoritarian governess. VALERIE is ill.*)

HARDWICK:I believe, Ma'am, that we are all born animal. Our task is to bring enlightenment, discipline and civilisation to souls otherwise lost in Hell.

VALERIE: I think you will find Anne does not reside in Hell, Mrs Hardwick.

ELIZABETH:I interpreted Mrs Hardwick as speaking metaphorically, Valerie.

HARDWICK:Indeed, your Ladyship, Hell is a condition in which one cannot come into God's light. Ignorance ensures this.

VALERIE: Let me make myself clear, Mrs Hardwick. I had no intention of hiring a governess for Anne. It is my failing health and the insistence of Mrs Goodwithy here that has persuaded me.

ELIZABETH:However, we are both agreed that Anne needs to be tutored in preparation for her Coming Out Ball.

VALERIE: Anne is someone who is used to being treated kindly, Mrs Hardwick.

HARDWICK:Without indulging the child, I'm sure.

(*ANNE bursts into the room in great distress.*)

ANNE: Grandma! Grandma!

(*ANNE throws herself onto VALERIE.*)

ELIZABETH:Anne, for goodness' sake!

VALERIE: Stop child, what is it?

ANNE: Jenkins and Dewey fight. Dewey going away.

VALERIE: Yes, I know. He asked for a job in the mill.

ANNE: You not let him go?

VALERIE: Why yes, of course.

ANNE: Bring him back!

HARDWICK:Excuse me.

ANNE: Who she?

VALERIE: This is Mrs Hardwick. She is to be your tutor.

HARDWICK:Good evening, Anne.

ANNE: (*makes a chimp-style grunt*) Go away!

VALERIE: Anne.

ELIZABETH:Anne, leave Valerie alone. She is not well.

ANNE: I tell Jenkins to get Dewey back but he not do it.

HARDWICK:Jenkins?

ELIZABETH:The gardener. Jenkins has been Anne's... guardian. Remarkable knowledge in some areas, complete blank in others.

VALERIE: Anne, please let go of me.

(*ANNE lets go.*)

ELIZABETH:There, I told you, Anne. You must learn to control yourself.

ANNE: Sorry, sorry. Me not hurt you.

VALERIE: I know, child, I know. I think I had better go. Elizabeth, can you assist me please?

ANNE: But grandma, what about Dewey?

VALERIE: People have to leave us occasionally, Anne. We are sad to see them go, of course, but that is the way of the world.

(*VALERIE and ELIZABETH make to exit.*)

ANNE: No, Dewey not go, Dewey not go!

(*ANNE throws a tantrum.*)

ELIZABETH:For goodness' sake, Anne. All this fuss. You have not made a very good impression on Mrs Hardwick. What must she be thinking? Excuse us, please. I shall return as soon as I can.

(*VALERIE and ELIZABETH exit.*)

HARDWICK:Well, well, well, so this is how chimpanzees behave, is it?

ANNE: No. (*as if HARDWICK is stupid*)

HARDWICK:Oh, I think it is. I think you are behaving like an animal. I see I shall have to tame you, my girl, tame you.

(*The chimpanzee BEN appears in the shadows. ANNE associates HARDWICK with BEN from this point on. HARDWICK, unlike ANNE, cannot see BEN although he works in close relation to her. BEN shepherds ANNE into HARDWICK'S clutches.*)

ANNE: I not like you.

HARDWICK:Sentiment is neither here nor there, child. Purpose is everything. Stand up straight.

ANNE: This is straight.

HARDWICK:Nonsense, child. Up. Up.

ANNE: Hurts.

HARDWICK:All lessons worth learning are painful, girl. From now on you are to stay away from Jenkins, do you hear me?

ANNE: No.

HARDWICK:You will soon learn to do as I say, child. Or you will feel the pain of your own wrongdoing.

(HARDWICK raises ANNE'S chin to pull her up straight. This is unnatural for ANNE and painful on her muscles. SOPHIE enters.)

SOPHIE: There you are.

(SOPHIE registers what HARDWICK is doing. HARDWICK stops immediately.)

SOPHIE: What is going on here? Who are you?

(ANNE, scared, runs to SOPHIE for comfort. BEN goes to HARDWICK'S side like an obedient dog. Lights down as the two groups stare at each other.)

(End of ACT ONE.)

Act Two

SCENE TWENTY-FIVE

(*The MUSIC HALL ARTISTE sings.*)
Ooh, ooh, ah-ah-ah!
My love's a chimpanzee,
And when she scratches her armpit,
It really tickles me.

But, oh, how she dreams of being accepted
By the ruling class
Then swings in a gown and raises a frown
When she shows her....

Ooh, ooh, ah-ah-ah!
My love's a chimpanzee,
You may think it lame to marry this dame
But there ain't no fleas on me.

(*The MUSIC HALL ARTISTE smiles wickedly and exits as the lights come up on ANNE in her ball gown. Music changes to a ballroom setting.*)

SCENE TWENTY-SIX

(*VALERIE, ELIZABETH and MRS HARDWICK enter with ball masks on sticks held over their faces.*

The masks are of African animals. They reveal who they are. Dancers process on in couples and are formally introduced to ANNE. They wear masks which are attached to their heads. ANNE reacts to the different pairs of animals. When SOPHIE is introduced she takes off her mask. ANNE is delighted to see her. They kiss. VALERIE is jealous and pulls ANNE back to greet her other guests. ELIZABETH and MRS HARDWICK watch over them.

Finally, a dashing man in a chimpanzee mask is introduced to ANNE. ANNE nervously takes her place to lead the polka with the man.

The scene needs to have a slightly surreal quality. The DANCERS are ruling-class guests, many of whom are here out of curiosity and are easily disposed to ridicule.

ANNE and her partner begin dancing. Everyone watches to see what she will do. The family are very tense. As ANNE does well so she relaxes and begins to enjoy herself. VALERIE smiles, ELIZABETH acknowledges, "so far, so good".

The DANCERS, many of whom have been waiting for ANNE to fail, applaud her and begin to whoop and call out. Their clapping becomes rythmic as the music quickens to a frantic pace. ANNE is hallucinating and becoming terrified.

A nightmare sequence follows in which the DANCERS become her predators, seeking to devour her. ANNE is raised up before being consumed by the group, who tear at her flesh. At the climax, the hallucination suddenly stops. The DANCERS resume their normal dancing positions as if nothing had happened (which in their minds, it has not). ANNE is behaving like a frightened chimpanzee. The guests are astonished. They begin laughing at ANNE. VALERIE is destroyed and angry. This is what ELIZABETH feared. HARDWICK expected no less and savours the *outcome. SOPHIE tries to help ANNE. AUGUSTA is humiliated.)*

SOPHIE: Anne, Anne, it's all right. Stop, stop.

(ANNE realises what is happening.)

ANNE: Grandma? Grandma, I sorry. I try again?

(The GUESTS all gossip and laugh.)

VALERIE: *(to her guests)* Leave my house. Please leave us.

ANNE: Grandma, I not do it again. I promise.

VALERIE: *(to ELIZABETH)* Get me away from here. Get me away.

ELIZABETH:What did you expect?

(As the last of the DANCERS leave, VALERIE descends to ANNE and slaps her fiercely across the face.)

VALERIE: Why!?

SOPHIE: Valerie!

ANNE: Me not mean it. Me not mean it.

SOPHIE: Of course you didn't.

(As SOPHIE comforts ANNE, VALERIE explodes with fury and pushes SOPHIE away from ANNE.)

VALERIE: Get away from her! Leave us!

(VALERIE collapses. AUGUSTA and ELIZABETH help her off.)

ELIZABETH:Oh, my God, quickly, get her to her room.

(HARDWICK waits as the room clears.)

HARDWICK:See what you've done, young lady? See what you've done? Your nasty, wilful little tantrum.

SOPHIE: Leave her alone. It was hardly her fault.

HARDWICK:I think you had better go, Miss Sophie.

ANNE: Sophie not go.

SOPHIE: Remember that you are a servant here, Mrs Hardwick.

(*ELIZABETH enters.*)

ELIZABETH:Do as Mrs Hardwick says, Sophie dear. Now, please.

ANNE: Sophie don't leave.

SOPHIE: Don't worry. I shan't be far away.

ANNE: No, Sophie stay. Sophie stay.

(*SOPHIE exits.*)

ELIZABETH:Have you seen what you've done? Your grandmother has collapsed. Have you finally destroyed her?

ANNE: I go see Grandma.

ELIZABETH:You keep away from her. Well, from now on you will be solely in the charge of Mrs Hardwick. You leave your grandmother in peace. For God's sake, what if she dies?

HARDWICK:I do believe you might have finally killed her, Anne. After she risked her health to find you, now you destroy her in public. Is that how you thank her?

ANNE: No, no.

HARDWICK:I think you had better start thinking of ways to make this better, don't you?

ANNE: I don't know any.

HARDWICK:Oh yes, you do. Think.

(*ANNE does so.*)

ANNE: Would it make it better if I never went to the greenhouse again? (*HARDWICK wants more.*) If I never saw Jenkins. Would that make things better?

HARDWICK:I would say that was the very least you could do. Why don't you attend to Lady Valerie, Mrs Good-withy. I believe Anne could make suggestions till dawn.

ELIZABETH:Yes, thank you. I shall.

(*ELIZABETH exits but not without some uneasse.*)

SCENE TWENTY-SEVEN

(*Lighting and sound become more threatening. [The scene is however, continuous from sc. 26, above.]*)

HARDWICK:Well now, Anne. What else can you suggest to make it better?

(*BEN appears. ANNE sees him.*)

ANNE: Sleep in my bed?

HARDWICK:Sleep in your bed.

(*ANNE stuggles for more ideas.*)

ANNE: I don't know anymore.

HARDWICK:Yes, you do. Think. What else is there? What else does God expect of you?

ANNE: Sit at table? Eat cooked food?

HARDWICK:With a...? With a...?

ANNE: With a knife and fork?

HARDWICK:These are the easy things, Anne. Little things. What are the difficult things you can do?

(*ANNE knows what she means. ALICE enters and bids ANNE to come with her.*)

ANNE: I never make chimp talk. Never walk chimp.

(The colony of chimpanzees make their way onstage and call gently to ANNE. All their movements are slowed and dreamlike.)

HARDWICK:More, Anne. There is more.

ANNE: No, there's not. I'm a good girl.

HARDWICK:There is more! And how dare you speak back to me!

ANNE: Never think chimpanzee.

(The CHIMPS are rejected and turn away, sitting unhappily.)

HARDWICK:Never think chimpanzee. But do you mean it, Anne? God needs to know that you mean it. Remember, he sees everything you do, every thought you have.

ANNE: Please tell him I not think chimpanzee.

(JENKINS enters and gestures as if saying the rhyme "There was a little man".)

ANNE: I never see Jenkins.

(JENKINS, rejected, loses heart and becomes still. DEWEY enters as if calling ANNE into his arms.)

ANNE: I never love... I never love....

(DEWEY, rejected, also becomes still.)

ANNE: Please, tell God, I don't want him looking at me.

HARDWICK: Because you know you are guilty of evil things, Anne, animal things.

(ANNE and DEWEY look at each other.)

ANNE: Yes.

(The music changes from a nightmare to something sexy and rhythmic. All the characters are swept into

*movement — a sensual release — with the exception of
HARDWICK, who watches ANNE. ANNE wraps
herself around DEWEY in a sexual movement. She
breaks away and as she moves amongst the creatures,
finds JENKINS and cuddles into him. Then ANNE
resumes a more sexual dance before the music cuts to
being a nightmare again. The characters continue the
movements in slowed motion.)*

HARDWICK:God can forgive you, Anne. We can all forgive
you. What does God want?

ANNE: God want me to obey him.

HARDWICK:Certainly, but more, Anne. What else must you
do to God?

ANNE: Love him.

HARDWICK:Love Him. And will you?

ANNE: Yes.

HARDWICK:You must work very hard, Anne, very hard to be
good. I will help you.

(*SOPHIE enters and gestures to ANNE to run away
with her.*)

HARDWICK:I alone, Anne.

(*SOPHIE is rejected.*

*Suddenly the colony senses danger as music
changes again with the entrance of the HUNTER with
a rifle. Their movements of panic are slowed down.*

*On one level of interpretation, this is a reenactment
of ANNE'S capture by the HUNTER, on another level,
she is killing everything dear to her. ALICE sees the
HUNTER and tries to protect her child, ANNE. The
HUNTER shoots ALICE. ANNE is distraught and
terrified.*

*JENKINS moves across to protect ANNE and he is
also shot. DEWEY, seeing his father slain, goes to him*

then turns for revenge on the *HUNTER who fires again, killing DEWEY.*

SOPHIE is ANNE'S last means of protection and shields ANNE from the bullet as the HUNTER shoots for the final time. SOPHIE falls dead at ANNE'S feet as have all those dear to her.)

HUNTER: It's all right, girl. I won't harm you.

(*The ghosts of ANNE'S parents, RUTH and GEOFFREY, enter with a net covered with "feminine" things like bows, dolls and ballet shoes. They place the net over ANNE, happy that she has been retrieved. ANNE is caught in the net and screams before "freezing" in an image of capture.*)

HARDWICK:Good girl, Anne. Good girl.

(*Lights down.*)

SCENE TWENTY-EIGHT

(*Lights up on TIMOTHY, VALERIE, ELIZABETH, AUGUSTA and SOPHIE in VALERIE'S study. DEWEY and JENKINS are in the greenhouse.*)

SOPHIE: It is so good to see you, Timmy. Did you get my letters? Why did you never reply? It was so mean....

TIMOTHY: My dear, Sophie. Why, still a spinster? How contrary a fate for a girl who thought of nothing else but marriage.

(*SOPHIE is hurt by this.*)

SOPHIE: We all change.

(*He is cold to AUGUSTA.*)

AUGUSTA: Timothy.

TIMOTHY: There have been times when I thought I would never see you again. You must have thought the same.

VALERIE: Perhaps we can pursue these touching scenes after I have spoken to Timothy?

SCENE TWENTY-NINE

(The greenhouse. JENKINS is depressed. It is awkward between the men.)

DEWEY: How come Anne don't come here no more?

JENKINS: I don't know. Perhaps she doesn't want to.

DEWEY: Hasn't anyone said?

JENKINS: Nothing.

DEWEY: Well, there's the thanks you get.

JENKINS: Don't start.

SCENE THIRTY

(HARDWICK and ANNE in a dance in which HARDWICK trains and physically manipulates ANNE. ANNE is more plainly dressed.)

SCENE THIRTY-ONE

(*TIMOTHY and VALERIE with ELIZABETH.*)

VALERIE: I have followed your progress. You have done well. An officer, no less.

TIMOTHY: I have followed your progress with similar interest.

VALERIE: And?

TIMOTHY: It is sad to see the mills doing so badly.

VALERIE: I am tired, Timothy. I need you to manage our affairs and oversee the disposal of the mills. The question is, do you wish to return to your family?

TIMOTHY: You had always groomed me for the task.

VALERIE: You betrayed my trust.

TIMOTHY: I have paid the price and won.

VALERIE: As I hoped you would.

TIMOTHY: In case Anne failed you?

(*Pause.*)

VALERIE: Anne will never be accepted in society. She needs someone strong to safeguard a secure future for her. Do you wish to resume your responsibilities to the family?

TIMOTHY: Nothing would give me greater pleasure than to return the debt my family owes you.

(*VALERIE looks to ELIZABETH as if giving her consent.*)

ELIZABETH: There are, of course, legal papers we would like you to sign. They lay out exactly what your responsibilities are and the limitations of your financial powers. Perhaps though, you would like to unpack first.

TIMOTHY: First? No, first I should like to see Anne. I hear from Sophie that she is quite a young lady.

(*ELIZABETH looks at VALERIE, suspecting that she has more than financial plans for TIMOTHY and ANNE.*)

SCENE THIRTY-TWO

(*The greenhouse. Some moments later.*)

DEWEY: You've heard about the mill, I suppose.

JENKINS: I told you.

DEWEY: We'll fight. They can't sack people and cut the other's wages.

JENKINS: Why? They've paid you. What else do they owe?

DEWEY: We'll see. Everyone's behind us.

JENKINS: Us? Who's us?

DEWEY: We've joined a union.

JENKINS: Look after yourself, Dewey. Never mind everyone else. They'll never be grateful and (*directed at DEWEY personally*) when you need them they're nowhere to be seen.

DEWEY: I get back as often as I can. (*pause*) How's the garden?

JENKINS: I don't know. The reason's gone out of it.

DEWEY: Anne will come back. She'll help. (*DEWEY knows this is unlikely.*) I suppose she's a young lady now, then?

JENKINS: She always was, Dewey. People can't change the shape they were born into. You can't either.

DEWEY: If you see her, tell her I was looking for her.

144

(*DEWEY makes to leave.*)

JENKINS: Wait. I've got you a basket of vegetables, take them back with you.

SCENE THIRTY-THREE

(*A resumption of the earlier dance, but HARDWICK can now manipulate ANNE'S movement without physical contact. TIMOTHY breaks the scene. Lights change to something more naturalistic.*)

SCENE THIRTY-FOUR

TIMOTHY: Well, well, well, our little chimpanzee.

(*ANNE is embarrassed.*)

HARDWICK:Greet your cousin, Anne.

ANNE: Cousin Timothy, how glad we all are to see you safe.

(*TIMOTHY is surprised.*)

TIMOTHY: My dear Anne, what a transformation. You are, quite.... Well, I am astonished. You shall show me the grounds. Many a night I have dreamt of the garden. How is Jenkins?

ANNE: I... I....

HARDWICK:Lady Anne has no concern for the well being of a gardener, Master Timothy.

TIMOTHY: Really? Well, nevertheless you will show me the gardens, won't you, Anne?

HARDWICK:Why Anne would be delighted, Master Timothy.

> (*ANNE grants TIMOTHY her hand and he leads her away.*)

TIMOTHY: What have they done to you, Anne? Cut out your tongue?

SCENE THIRTY-FIVE

> (*Continues from the previous scene. VALERIE, ELIZABETH and AUGUSTA join HARDWICK and TIMOTHY in a brief resumption of dance to show them manipulating ANNE. TIMOTHY is now central to the dance.*)

SCENE THIRTY-SIX

> (*SOPHIE rushes in and the scene returns to naturalism. The family are gathered in a room.*)

SOPHIE: Stop it! Stop it! Leave her alone for goodness' sake.

VALERIE: I beg your pardon, Sophie dear, did I hear you knock?

AUGUSTA: Go back out and knock, Sophie.

SOPHIE: (*to AUGUSTA*) I will not. (*to VALERIE*) I'm not playing your little games. I want this to stop.

ELIZABETH:What precisely do you refer to, Sophie?

SOPHIE: Your treatment of Anne. Look at her. You are destroying her.

(ELIZABETH can see that this is true.)

VALERIE: Anne, are you happy?

ANNE: Yes, grandmother, quite happy.

SOPHIE: I know you are not. Anne, come to the greenhouse with me. We'll see Jenkins. Your rose is in bloom, have you seen it? It is you. Very beautiful. Come with me now. Come on.

VALERIE: Anne is perfectly free to go to the greenhouse any time she wishes. Anne, would you like to go?

ANNE: No.

SOPHIE: What they have done to you is invisible, isn't it? You destroy yourself.

ELIZABETH:Sophie, dear, we all need to restrain ourselves, otherwise chaos would preside.

HARDWICK:Indeed, Miss Sophie, perhaps your education is not quite complete.

SOPHIE: I would never let you get your hands on me, I assure you, for fear that I would end up as twisted out of shape by denial as you sad women.

VALERIE: Sophie! That is enough!

AUGUSTA: I don't pretend to understand what you are referring to, Sophie, but your tone is quite unnecessary.

VALERIE: As it happens, Sophie, you have just ruined what was a very pleasant occasion. Perhaps you would like to hear the news?

TIMOTHY: Over the past few months since my return, cousin Anne has been kind enough to spend many hours with me. During that time I believe we have come to admire each other greatly.

SOPHIE: No. Anne, you cannot. I know who you love.

(ELIZABETH is concerned by this remark and goes to

ANNE'S side as SOPHIE continues. ANNE has never seen such sympathy in ELIZABETH before, she is uneasy with it.)

SOPHIE: The rose is still blooming. Anne... Oh this is wonderful, isn't it? Of course, no wonder you are all so happy. Valerie, if they marry, Timothy will run the estate in Anne's best interests. Mother, your dream come true. Timothy, you finally get your hands on the wealth and Elizabeth, ah, now then Elizabeth, what do you get, Valerie?

(ELIZABETH pulls away from ANNE, embarrassed.)

VALERIE: You will withdraw that remark or leave my house.

SOPHIE: I shall stay as long as Anne wants me to.

VALERIE: Oh, really? Anne, Sophie has behaved outrageously and hurt us all greatly, I have asked her to leave the house. Do you agree?

ANNE: Yes, Sophie, you must go.

SOPHIE: No, you don't mean that.

ANNE: Go Sophie. You must go.

(ELIZABETH cannot condone VALERIE'S behaviour any longer.)

ELIZABETH:*(in disgust)* Excuse me.

VALERIE: *(indignantly)* Elizabeth!

(ELIZABETH exits. Lights out on the scene.)

SCENE THIRTY-SEVEN

(Lights up on an early morning exterior. JENKINS calls to unseen men as five swings, mounted sideways,

148

are lowered into the space. They are to be regarded as horses.)

JENKINS: You men run the dogs along the side of the valley and down towards the river.

TIM: (*entering*) All set, Jenkins?

JENKINS: Aye, Master Timothy. The men are ready for the off.

(*JENKINS "foots" TIMOTHY into his saddle so that he sits astride the swing, facing forward. AUGUSTA and MRS HARDWICK enter and are helped onto their horses. They ride side saddle.*)

TIMOTHY: I hear your son has been making a nuisance of himself. That's a shame, Jenkins. It seems he is leading a futile strike against the family. What, I wonder, are your opinions on the matter?

AUGUSTA: Oh, opinions, opinions, why must we have opinions? Every opinion a person holds has cost them dear. Personally, I see no need of them at all! Jenkins, hurry along.

JENKINS: (*amused*) Aye, Ma'am.

TIMOTHY: Mother, do not intervene in my discussions with employees.

(*ANNE enters nervously.*)

TIMOTHY: Anne, are you ready?

ANNE: Yes.

TIMOTHY: No need to look so scared. The fox does not kill us.

(*ELIZABETH enters as ANNE is helped onto her horse.*)

ELIZABETH:Good morning. Lady Valerie wishes us all good hunting.

(*ELIZABETH sees her chance to speak with ANNE.*)

HARDWICK:It's a fine morning for it.

ELIZABETH:Anne, before it is too late, this marriage to Timothy... do you really want it?

ANNE: It is good.

ELIZABETH:But it is what you want?

ANNE: I want what is good.

ELIZABETH:Anne, if you love someone but cannot have them it is a terrible thing, but to have someone that you do not love is worse. Believe me, I've known both.

ANNE: I love everyone by doing this.

ELIZABETH:Everyone but yourself, perhaps. Is this what we have done to you?

(*ANNE turns away. ELIZABETH leaves her and is helped onto her horse.*)

TIMOTHY: Jenkins, the hounds!

(*JENKINS brings on the hounds. As we hear them approaching they sound like dogs but the sound changes as they enter to that of chimpanzees. ANNE sees them as chimpanzees and is disturbed.*)

JENKINS: Good morning, Lady Anne.

ANNE: Jenkins!

JENKINS: Yes, Ma'am?

HARDWICK:Ready, Anne?

ANNE: Yes.

(*JENKINS exits.*)

TIMOTHY: And now, we're off!

(*The chase is on. ANNE is distraught. Music captures the spirit of the movement. The actors swing out across the stage. Perhaps the swings can be rigged so that TIMOTHY and ANNE swing out over the audience.*)

The CHIMPANZEES exaggerate their forward movement by slowing it down. Suddenly, DEWEY rushes out in front of TIMOTHY.)

DEWEY: Hold up there! Hold up!

TIMOTHY: What are you doing, man. I could have run you down!

DEWEY: Master, we need to speak.

ANNE: Dewey!

DEWEY: Miss Anne, I hear congratulations are in order.

TIMOTHY: Oh, it's you. Get out of our way.

DEWEY: You won't speak to us so what choice do I have?

TIMOTHY: I said, get out of our way.

DEWEY: We've got people starving in the town. Starving!

TIMOTHY: If you do not get out of my way I will ride you down. Do you understand?

DEWEY: Go ahead, you might as well. I'd rather go this way than starve to death under your table.

TIMOTHY: Have it your own way.

(TIMOTHY whips DEWEY. The action is stylised. JENKINS runs on.)

ANNE: Timothy, no!

JENKINS: Get your hands off him.

(JENKINS grabs TIMOTHY'S whip and strikes him as he speaks.)

JENKINS: You don't go treating people like that! You got to learn, you don't treat people like that!

(JENKINS stops, then realises what he has done. TIMOTHY grabs the whip from his hand.)

TIMOTHY: Get off my land. Never set foot here again.

(*JENKINS turns to DEWEY and helps him up.*)

JENKINS: You all right, boy?

DEWEY: Aye.

(*They exit past ANNE. She is very upset.*)

AUGUSTA: (*to TIMOTHY*) My poor child, are you hurt?

TIMOTHY: Nothing will ruin this day, nothing. We ride on.

ELIZABETH:Wouldn't it be better to turn back?

HARDWICK:No, Ma'am, it would confuse the men. We must continue.

(*ANNE leaps into a gallop. They chase after her.*)

TIMOTHY: Anne?! Anne?!

(*The hunt continues and builds up quickly.*)

TIMOTHY: A kill! A kill!

(*A CHIMP rears up before dying. The other chimps gather round the corpse. The riders dismount. ELIZABETH, AUGUSTA and MRS HARDWICK exit. TIMOTHY shoos the chimps away except for BEN who takes a bite from the chimpanzee's flesh. TIMOTHY sees BEN off then dips his hand into the blood and approaches ANNE.*)

TIMOTHY: Come now, Anne. You must be bloodied.

(*TIMOTHY smears the blood onto ANNE'S face. She is petrified and runs, climbing high. TIMOTHY and BEN pursue. ANNE comes to a 'precipice'. As the males close in ANNE jumps and lands in the arms of the chimpanzees. Lights snap out as ANNE falls.*)

SCENE THIRTY-EIGHT

(*Lights up on a distraught VALERIE with ELIZA-BETH.*)

152

VALERIE: All for nothing. Fourteen years of searching. Fourteen years. And then, worrying, struggling to bring her into humanity, indulging her, bending the rules, giving more freedom than I ever had. And she destroys herself. How I wish I had done the same many, many years ago. Think of the pain I would have spared myself. What did she think? That our love and sacrifice was meaningless? That it could just be tossed into a river and swept down stream along with her?! How little I knew her. How little I meant. What a fool I am. People don't love you. They just fool you whilst they get what they want.

ELIZABETH:Anne loved you. Of course she did.

VALERIE: She could have done, you never let her. At least with Timothy I know precisely where I stand. He has never known my love and he has become my natural heir.

ELIZABETH:I am not staying to listen to this self-pitying bile.

VALERIE: Perhaps you would if I raised your wages.

ELIZABETH:Valerie, rant all you want to, but do not insult my integrity! You indulged Anne with all of your love. No one else was ever considered.

VALERIE: You see, you were jealous.

ELIZABETH:You loved her because you wanted her to be like you. She is not to blame for that. Has it occurred to you that your love was part of the reason for her suicide? That I could understand.

VALERIE: My love? My love?

ELIZABETH:(*retracting*) All of us.

VALERIE: My love is poison? What do you know of my love?

ELIZABETH:What indeed?

VALERIE: My love is poison, is that what you are saying? The child was incapable of love. If she had loved me she would not have killed herself. It is not my love that did that, it was her lack of humanity!

ELIZABETH:Humanity, what a term. It covers so many posi-bilities. You can bemoan the lack of love in your life, Valerie. And indeed, you are a sorry sight, a woman about to die and she is surrounded by people who are paid to be there.

VALERIE: Stop it.

ELIZABETH:And yet the potential for love was all around her. You have only yourself to blame. You have wanted it like this. You have enjoyed your power. I do not feel sorry for you. You have spurned every possible relationship where love could have been found.

VALERIE: Where? Where? Augusta? Sophie?

ELIZABETH:Me?

(*VALERIE turns away from ELIZABETH. The sting has gone from their argument.*)

VALERIE: You are going to leave me, aren't you?

ELIZABETH:Yes, I think I must whilst I still have some life left.

VALERIE: I have loved you.

ELIZABETH:Then what a waste of both our lives this has been.

(*TIMOTHY enters. ELIZABETH goes.*)

TIMOTHY: Sorry, should I have waited?

VALERIE: No. I name you as my successor. You must preserve the estate. You have proven your abilities beyond question.

TIMOTHY: I shall not fail the family.

(*Pause.*)

154

VALERIE: Did you love Anne?

TIMOTHY: No.

VALERIE: Then you are lucky, you do not feel this hatred for her now!

(*Lights down.*)

SCENE THIRTY-NINE

(*The CHIMPS appear and take up positions around the set at various levels. Music suggesting an industrial Hell fills the air as the CHIMPS change their shapes to become industrial workers operating machines. They strain with the effort.*

SOPHIE appears, dressed as a suffragette. She is handing out political leaflets in the street. DEWEY crosses the stage. He is huddled. He wears one of ANNE'S roses in his lapel. As DEWEY enters, the music stops and the CHIMPS "freeze" in their positions.)

SOPHIE: Wait, you there! Wait! Excuse me, but can I ask you where you got that rose?

(*DEWEY turns.*)

SOPHIE: Dewey? Dewey Jenkins?

DEWEY: Miss Sophie. What you doing here?

SOPHIE: Would you like a leaflet?

DEWEY: All right.

SOPHIE: How are you? (*no reply*) Have you work?

DEWEY: I'm blacklisted, Ma'am.

SOPHIE: And your father?

155

DEWEY: Father's not so well, Miss.

SOPHIE: Anne's death must have shocked him greatly.

DEWEY: Aye, Ma'am.

SOPHIE: She loved you, did you know that?

DEWEY: She told you that?

SOPHIE: She wanted to name her rose after you. That is it, isn't it?

DEWEY: Aye, Ma'am. All we got left.

SOPHIE: She gave it to you?

DEWEY: Yes.

SOPHIE: You knew then?

DEWEY: Yes, she told me.

(*SOPHIE is pleased.*)

SOPHIE: Would it be possible... could I have a cutting or something, that I could grow? It would mean a great deal to me.

DEWEY: You'd better come with me.

(*They cross the stage to where JENKINS sits slumped in a chair. The CHIMPS hold their positions.*)

SCENE FORTY

(*Lights up on JENKINS looking very frail in a chair.*)

SOPHIE: The world has changed, all right.

JENKINS: Lights on all night, don't matter if you work day or night. Children born into this, they think its natural, you know. I don't understand the children no more. Time to go.

DEWEY: I'm trying to work a passage to America, Miss, see if we can't start a new life there.

JENKINS: People can think, can't they? We can think new things, new ways of doing things.

SOPHIE: Yes, yes we can.

JENKINS: Then, who thought of doing it this way?

SOPHIE: People adapt.

JENKINS: So do roses but I wouldn't breed a hybrid that never bloomed.

DEWEY: Miss Sophie wanted a cutting from Anne's rose.

JENKINS: Wrong time of year.

SOPHIE: Oh.

DEWEY: I think we should let her.

JENKINS: No.

DEWEY: Maybe she can help us.

JENKINS: Dewey!

(*DEWEY goes into another room – offstage.*)

SOPHIE: I'm sorry to find you so unwell. (*pause*) Do you ever go back to the estate?

JENKINS: Do you?

SOPHIE: No.

JENKINS: No.

SOPHIE: Anne would have wanted to thank you. It was you who let her be human. She taught me a lot.

JENKINS: Like what?

SOPHIE: That we can all change our shape.

JENKINS: Can we?

(*DEWEY enters.*)

DEWEY: Miss Sophie.

(*ANNE enters. She is five or six months pregnant.*)

ANNE: Hello, Sophie.

(*Lights out.*)

SCENE FORTY-ONE

(*VALERIE and TIMOTHY are in the study. JAC-QUELINE and AUGUSTA stand below as if outside the study.*)

TIMOTHY: If what they say is true, she is pregnant with Dewey Jenkins' child. It seems they have been living in squalor in Albert Street.

VALERIE: What do they want from me?

TIMOTHY: My guess would be money.

VALERIE: Of course money, but how much?

TIMOTHY: Anne might ask for the estate.

(*VALERIE and TIMOTHY exit the study. JACQUE-LINE sees VALERIE and assists her to a chiar. AUGUSTA seizes her opportunity.*)

AUGUSTA: Is it true that Sophie is coming here today?

VALERIE: So we believe.

AUGUSTA: Why was I not informed? Why must I hear these things from servants?

TIMOTHY: Sophie is here with Anne.

AUGUSTA: Then I demand to see her.

TIMOTHY: This is a business matter.

AUGUSTA: A business matter? This is a mother's matter and none of your business.

TIMOTHY: Very well, stay and then leave us. (*to JAC-QUELINE*) Show them in.

(*ANNE walks towards VALERIE. AUGUSTA goes to embrace SOPHIE.*)

AUGUSTA: Sophie, dear!

SOPHIE: Mama.

(*SOPHIE is cool towards AUGUSTA who is hurt by this.*)

VALERIE: Anne. How cruel of you to put us through such grief.

ANNE: I did not know my own mind. I was saved by Dewey and stayed with him.

VALERIE: Did we deserve such cold-hearted abuse?

ANNE: I'm not sure.

AUGUSTA: Anne!

VALERIE: You were engaged to Timothy, have you nothing to say to him?

ANNE: Hello, Timothy. You look very good.

VALERIE: So tell us, why have you come back now?

ANNE: I wish to claim my inheritance upon your death.

VALERIE: I will not allow it.

SOPHIE: I have checked this, Valerie, it is Anne's right.

VALERIE: Anne is dead.

AUGUSTA: Nonsense, Valerie, she's standing right in front of you.

VALERIE: Anne died in the jungle, aged two, alongside her parents, Geoffrey and Ruth. A girl was found years later but she proved to be an imposter. She was so clearly not a Brecknor. She had no love of her family.

ANNE: I am Anne. Please do not take that away from me.

VALERIE: Do you think I want to? Do you think this does not hurt me? Anne, even at this late stage if you were to come to me, hold me, I would forgive you. You can come back and live in the house.

ANNE: And my baby?

VALERIE: No, not that, but we will care for it, find a good home.

ANNE: I want to give birth, be human. I do not want your money for myself.

TIMOTHY: Then who do you want it for?

ANNE: To end the misery of other people's lives. To let them be human.

TIMOTHY: Do you intend to run the estate as a charity?

ANNE: Until that day, when I thought I had died, I had never seen beyond these walls. Grandmother, you have shaped the world and it does not fit. Though I loved you, you are evil and I will change the shape of it.

VALERIE: I did find you too late. It is clear to me now that you were and are a cruel animal. Your mind has been tortured by your early experiences. Look at you, you try to commit suicide. When you fail you keep your life a secret from those who mourn your death. Then, in the midst of this insanity you live out of wedlock with a mill worker, displaying your irresponsible disregard for society's morals, and now we hear you are pregnant. You are not fit to be a mother, can't you see that? If not you, then we have a responsibility to that child. You shall be committed to an asylum for the well being of you both.

           (*ANNE is terrified. ANNE resorts to chimp sounds.*)

SOPHIE: She will not go!

TIMOTHY: The arrangements are already made.

SOPHIE: She is sane and you know it!

AUGUSTA: Valerie, no.

VALERIE: We are her family. We have to do what is best for each other.

AUGUSTA: Everything. You destroy everything, everything we could be.

VALERIE: (*dismissive*) Augusta.

SOPHIE: Anne, stay with me. I will fetch Dewey.

TIMOTHY: Dewey is in police custody along with his father. They have been charged with common assault.

ANNE: No. Prison kill Jenkins. Give Dewey back to me! You keep the estate.

(*VALERIE and TIMOTHY share a look. Perhaps this is what they wanted to hear. VALERIE goes towards ANNE. It appears as if she is going to be kind.*)

VALERIE: How can we trust you? When we have given you everything and yet you hate us!

(*Music as TIMOTHY advances on ANNE. A dance as ANNE struggles to get away. SOPHIE, AUGUSTA and JACQUELINE exit. The cage is lowered to the ground. VALERIE opens the cage door. At the end of the dance TIMOTHY puts ANNE in the cage and VALERIE closes and locks it.*

ANNE pleads with VALERIE who walks away. ANNE descends into madness. ALICE enters and ANNE reaches out to her and is comforted. ANNE reverts to chimpanzee.

As the other CHIMPS enter to take up positions around the stage, DEWEY and JENKINS come onto the green-house stage as convicts. Their hands are tied behind their backs. ANNE sees them.)

> *BESSIE approaches the cage and greets ANNE as SOPHIE and AUGUSTA enter holding ANNE'S BABY. SOPHIE goes to the cage and shows ANNE the BABY. ALICE looks over SOPHIE'S shoulder at the BABY as ANNE reaches out to stroke its face. Proud and brave, ANNE names the child.*

ANNE: Gwydion.

> *(ANNE strokes SOPHIE'S face as if to thank her. SOPHIE stands and returns to AUGUSTA'S side as VALERIE, TIMOTHY and BEN enter and observe ANNE in the cage. Then ELIZABETH enters and looks over the scene. Finally, the ghosts of ANNE'S parents enter and observe. ANNE looks around her then comes to face forward, clutching the bars of her cage. Music reaches its climax and the lights fade.)*

(THE END.)

Frida and Diego

A Love Story

Frida and Diego – A Love Story, was originally commissioned by Red Shift Theatre Company in 1989. The initial production was Directed by Jonathan Holloway, Designed by Charlotte Humpston, with Music by Adrian Johnston and Liam Grundy. The production premiered at the Assembly Rooms, Edinburgh on August 13th 1989 and won a Fringe First Award. Subsequent productions include the Stages Theatre, Houston; City College, San Francisco and the Stockolm's Stadsteater in 1993/94 (they subsequently toured Mexico with the play in 1995). The script was rewritten for production by the Mid Powys Youth Theatre in October 1994 at the Wyeside Arts Centre, Builth Wells. This production was Directed by Greg Cullen with Music by Steven Byrne, Design by Steve Fieldhouse, Costume Design by Allie Saunders. It is this script which is published here. The MPYT production was selected for the BT National Connections at the Royal National Theatre and performed at the Cottesloe in July, 1995.

The text is based upon the paintings of Frida Kahlo and Diego Rivera and how their lives and times combined to produce certain images. The play therefore demands that images from the paintings be realised in any production. In addition, I have attempted to employ a variety of styles and conventions which correspond to those the painters used. For example, a soliloquy mirrors a self-portrait, and poetry reflects the visual poetry of the artists. In terms of style the play ranges from realistic dialogue where the accent is firmly upon subtext, to naivety and on into an agit-prop *largesse*. These again mirror styles employed by Frida and Diego.

163

To fully realise the play, the shifts of style and convention must be marked because they indicate the emotional and attitudinal graph of the artists and their times. Indeed, Frida and Diego summon scenes from their past quite consciously in order to debate and reconcile their relationship. In this way form and content marry.

I was further concerned with exploring the Mexican view of Duality, a concept or perception of reality, which dates back to the Aztec religion. "From death comes life" is a common sentiment which finds expression in the form of the Calavera (see the work of J.G. Posada.) The Calaveras parody life though they could be, as one reviewer put it, dancing on Frida's coffin. Sinister and otherworldly the Calaveras most definitely are, but in Mexico papier-mache skeletons are figures of fun, symbols of Fiesta, playful reminders from a close friend of one's own mortality. Thus there are contradictions in the characters as well as in the themes expressed.

I have subtitled the play "A love story" not simply because of Frida and Diego's relationship but also because of their relationships with themselves, their art, their people and with life itself. They had many strongly felt wants and embodied within these wants is the desire not to have to want anymore, to wish you had never started wanting in the first place. "Duality" makes things whole rather than singular and isolated as in our dominant perception. To describe love as good and hate as bad is to deny love a wholeness. If one loves as strongly as Frida and Diego did one cannot help but suffer greatly from betrayal, woundings and death. To really love means at times wishing one no longer loved, that one had never started loving in the first place.

Notes on Staging the Play

The play should be treated as a "Dream play", psychically fluid and uncluttered by realistic settings. The entire play can take place as if in the mural 'A Dream of a Sunday Afternoon in the Alameda Park'. In some productions a backdrop of the Alameda Park, minus the characters, was painted, in others the mural was projected onto a plain backcloth. Projections of other paintings have been used to set scenes to great effect, and were used during Frida's exhibition.

The worst mistakes have been made when productions have tried to realistically create each location or treated the play as documentary. They destroyed the fluency of associations in the characters' minds which prompt scene to flow into scene.

Stage right is predominantly Frida's and stage left, Diego's. The sun and the moon. The central area, or the entire stage, can be used for larger locations. Thematically, dividing the stage in two emphasises the theme of duality in all things. Practically, it allows simultaneous scenes to be played without confusion of location.

The characters are Calaveras of actual people, therefore they are re-enacting events. This provides the director with the potential to employ stylised conventions such as mime; designers, the opportunity to see every object as unreal and allows actors to suggest locations.

One production took the notion of papier-mâché Calaveras and Judas from Mexican Folk Art and made every prop, including guns, in that naive and fantastical style. It helped create a world for the play whilst at the same time extending the theme of creativity as essential to living.

CHARACTERS

Diego Rivera
Frida Kahlo
Calavera Catarina
(Calavera Catarina is a death figure originally drawn by J.G. Posada, deployed again by Diego in 'A Dream of a Sunday Afternoon in the Alameda Park'. Catarina is a Calavera of a fashionable woman circa 1890. She is a comic figure, but also suggests, more sinisterly, death. In large cast productions Catarina has two young Calaveras with her as assistants. In Mexico 'Death' is sometimes referred to as 'the aunt of the little girls'.)

Senora Kahlo (Frida's mother)
Senor Kahlo (Frida's father)
Angelina Beloff (Diego's first wife)
Lupe Marin (Diego's second wife)
David Alfaro Siqueiros (A muralist and communist
                    revolutionary)
Ella Wolfe (A New York, Jewish, American revolutionary)
Bertram Wolfe (Ella's husband and Diego's biographer)
Alejandro Gomez Arias (Frida's first serious lover)
Policeman
Indian Family
Soldier
Scientist 1
Scientist 2
Nurse
Doctor
Mary
A Ford car worker
Dr Eloesser (Frida's gay doctor whilst in San Francisco)
Helen Wills-Moody (US Tennis champion)

Flores Sanchez
Lucienne Bloch
Arthur Neindorff
Stephan Dimitrioff (Diego's assistants on the mural 'Man at
                    the Cross-roads')
Cristina Kahlo (Frida's sister)
Leon Trotsky (Russian revolutionary and founder of
                the Red Army)
Natalia Trotsky (Leon's wife)

Calaveras (they adopt characters, otherwise they are like a
                chorus)

Act One
SCENE ONE

(*It is the morning after FRIDA KAHLO'S death. From blackout, a light slowly reveals DIEGO RIVERA standing alone and bereft. He holds a paint brush in the palm of one hand and gazes at it intently. His worn cotton worker's jacket, voluminous trousers and heavy boots hang from his weary body and root him to the ground. He looks from the paintbrush to the audience before putting the paintbrush in his jacket pocket and speaking to them.*)

DIEGO: We shall walk in the Alameda Park and dream
                                   a little.
There the trees ebb and flow like curtains
Impatient to be drawn across a stage.
There a moment is not an instant, isolated, lost,
                              without cousins,
But a prism through which all history can be
                    focused and cast onto a surface.

(*The speech is continuous as lights build behind DIEGO revealing the cast, all of whom are CALAVERAS, depticting characters from DIEGO'S mural, 'A Dream of a Sunday Afternoon in the Alameda Park'. FRIDA is missing.*)

DIEGO: Here we stand arrayed before you to take the bow.

(*Only CALAVERA CATARINA moves. She speaks to DIEGO and to us whilst taking him by the arm.*

167

DIEGO is enchanted and gladdened by the transformation. His characters are like old friends.)

CATARINA: The pickpocket and the bourgeoisie
The Indians and the Dictator's Police
Balloon sellers and liberationists
Rubbing shoulders with the inquisition's victim.

DIEGO: Betrayers and betrayed
Rise up to bow and beg the question
What now?
For last night our brave Cauhtemoc died.

CATARINA: And today we need to dream in the Alameda Park.

(*DIEGO agrees. The mural comes alive as the characters sing an acappella rendition of an organ pipe waltz. They promenade. DIEGO and CATARINA join them, greeting others as they stoll through the park, then they waltz. DIEGO is intoxicated, forgetful of his loss. Unseen by DIEGO, FRIDA enters accompanied by CALAVERAS.*)

DIEGO: (*joking to audience*) I seem to have walked beside death all my life.

FRIDA: Hey! Fatso!

(*CATARINA signals and the CALAVERAS freeze back into their depiction of the mural, this time with Frida in place. DIEGO approaches her.*)

DIEGO: What will I do without my Friducita?
In my eyes, last night they took Cauhtemoc's life
And now Montezuma can but sit and wait himself
to die,
And helpless, watch the conqueror,
Our images and temples downcast
And from the ruins build a new image of the past.
Thus by sword and thought hold power.
Which way now?

(*FRIDA comes to life.*)

FRIDA: From death comes life.

            (*DIEGO hugs FRIDA. The CALAVERAS come to life; they enjoy this reunion.*)

DIEGO: Help me to believe that. Tell me that we didn't waste our lives. That there is a future. That you don't regret me. Could I have saved you?

FRIDA: Ssh. I wanted to fly, but they only gave me straw wings.

DIEGO: Why can't we feel just one thing at a time? Just one thing purely? Last night, when she (CATARINA) took you, I wanted only to feel remorse, to rage and scream and folding inwards disappear. And yet I also felt relief. It makes me sick, but I feel relief. Do you hate me?

FRIDA: There are so many things. Trying to cluster them all together in one place is like herding sheep into a field with no fence. Far better to paint!

DIEGO: Yes.

FRIDA: And we shall love.

DIEGO: Very definitely.

FRIDA: And laugh.

DIEGO: And sing!

FRIDA: And tell stories.

DIEGO: I never lie!

FRIDA: And fight.

DIEGO: I knew when you came to see me at the Education building, that I would always love you!

            (*CATARINA signals and the CALAVERAS burst into a celebratory dance, reorganising themselves in a depiction of the Education Buiding mural, 'Our Bread'.*)

SCENE TWO

(DIEGO takes his paintbrush and mimes painting the figures. FRIDA goes to collect a series of empty picture frames. They re-enact the scene.)

FRIDA: Hey fatso!

(DIEGO turns to see who this offensive person is.)

DIEGO: Yes, "young lady"?

FRIDA: Come down off your scaffold. I have brought some paintings with me. I want honest opinion, no flattery and no funny business. I've been told all about you. All I want to know is, am I wasting my time? I have no training, I need to know.

DIEGO: I've seen you somewhere before.

FRIDA: No, you haven't.

DIEGO: Yes I have.

FRIDA: It's old age playing tricks.

DIEGO: Back at the Prepatoria! You were that brat who blew up Antonio Casso's lecture hall.

FRIDA: It was an accident!

DIEGO: It was a bomb!

FRIDA: It was a firecracker. I didn't know it would... it was an accident.

DIEGO: Do you have any more "accidents" planned?

FRIDA: No, you're safe.

DIEGO: What, even if I don't like your paintings? Well?

(FRIDA holds the frames so as to frame herself. Behind each one she strikes a different pose from a self-portrait. Between posing as her paintings, FRIDA is anxious and vulnerable. DIEGO grunts in response to them, giving away little of his true thoughts. He even enjoys increasing her anxiety. He sees the last painting.)

FRIDA: Well, am I wasting my time or not?

DIEGO: No. No, you are not. Have you any more like these?

FRIDA: At home.

DIEGO: Can I come and see them?

FRIDA: You mean it? (*trying to be casual*) You can visit me on Sunday. The Blue House on Londres Street, Coyoacán.

DIEGO: Sunday.

FRIDA: You really like them?

DIEGO: They are beautiful. There is a lot to do of course. Have you ever thought of painting a mural?

FRIDA: I have a sick hoof. A bus crash. I cannot stand for long.

           (*FRIDA collects her work.*)

DIEGO: Can I help?

FRIDA: No! ...You will come on Sunday?

DIEGO: Two o'clock?

FRIDA: Yes. (*pause*) Goodbye comrade.

DIEGO: Goodbye.

           (*She walks away, but shouts back:*)

FRIDA: I think you are the greatest painter in the world!

SCENE THREE

(*Lighting returns to the Park. The CALAVERAS stop depicting the painting and enjoy the lovers' happiness.*)

171

DIEGO: I wanted to throw down my brushes and run straight after you.

FRIDA: Even when I was a schoolgirl, I knew that one day I would marry you, have your children and bathe you. (*to audience*) It just took a while to persuade him.

(*FRIDA and DIEGO kiss.*)

SCENE FOUR

(*A red light comes up on Senora and Senor Kahlo in his dark room. He is developing a photograph of the happy couple. We may see it projected behind them.*)

S. KAHLO: This is the marriage of an elephant and a dove! She'll have nothing to wear. People will know we are bankrupt!

KAHLO: She plans to borrow Indian clothes from a maid.

S. KAHLO: I've worked all of my life not to wear Indian clothes. Now she chooses to wear them!

FRIDA: (*to audience*) My mother. You will have to excuse her.

S. KAHLO: She is doing this to punish me! Look at him, a communist, a divorcee, a non-believer! He has government money pouring out of his pockets! But us...? Where is the justice in this revolution! You, a master photographer, have no work, but him, he works always!

KAHLO: Who wants a photograph of their family these days? It would be full of empty spaces.

S. KAHLO: See, when we had a dictator the world was normal. Look at it now. How can she marry an old fat man?

KAHLO: They say he is the greatest muralist since Michelangelo.

S. KAHLO: In my days if you were unmarriageable you just made soup for the old ones. You didn't have to get into bed with them! Alejandro was such a nice boy. After polio she was lucky to get him. He even stayed constant after the accident. She could have had him... maybe. But Diego Rivera, he just wants young flesh, he probably doesn't care if it's crippled! (*blessing herself guiltily*) She is a saint.

(*SNR KAHLO appears to hang up the photograph he has been developing to dry. They both look at it. I suggest that all that activity be mimed.*)

S. KAHLO: Couldn't you have moved them into the shade a little?

KAHLO: My dear, I have never sought to improve upon that which God has chosen to make ugly.

S. KAHLO: Ugly? I could never take my eyes off her.

KAHLO: That is intelligence looking at you.

S. KAHLO: (*dissmisive*) Pah!

KAHLO: (*to himself*) But what would you know?

S. KAHLO: You won't see your little favourite again now. She is well provided for. But me? I have to sell my house, move out! Well, you can tell her that I cannot attend this civil wedding. If God cannot bless it, neither can I! Well? Do something! Tell her! Get her to stop! And don't forget, I'll be listening.

SCENE FIVE

(SENORA KAHLO stands as if by a window, whilst her husband goes down as if into the garden. FRIDA and DIEGO are kissing and groping with passion. SNR KAHLO is embarrassed.)

KAHLO: Don Diego Rivera.

(They are too engrossed to notice. He looks up to the window; his wife eggs him on.)

KAHLO: *(louder)* Don Diego Rivera.

(They hear him this time. They adjust their clothing.)

DIEGO: Don Guillermo Kahlo.

(DIEGO overheartily hugs frail SNR KAHLO.)

KAHLO: My daugher. I see that you are interested in her.

DIEGO: Erm... yes. *(to FRIDA)* Excuse us one moment.

(FRIDA, knowing what will be said, leaves the men and goes to join her mother in the house.)

KAHLO: She is not pretty.

DIEGO: Hmm.

(KAHLO looks up at the window. His wife encourages him on.)

KAHLO: She brings no wealth.

DIEGO: Ah, yes, I was meaning to have a word with you about that.

(FRIDA enters the room.)

KAHLO: You were?

S. KAHLO: Blood sucker! *(The men cannot hear her.)*

DIEGO: With your permission I will be joining your family.

S. KAHLO: Family? He is not the same species.

DIEGO: I hope you will not consider this presumptuous. Frida has told me of your financial difficulties. If you would allow it I would like to pay off your mortgage. That way you can stay in the Blue House. Frida loves Coyoacán and it would give me great pleasure to see you all secure again.

KAHLO: It would? (*He looks to his wife who is now in shock. SNR KAHLO decides to continue.*) You know Frida is the devil in disguise, don't you? The devil.

S.KAHLO: Wait!

KAHLO: She has always been this way, possessed!

DIEGO: Yes, I know.

KAHLO: And you accept this condition?

DIEGO: I do.

(SENORA KAHLO is greatly relieved, but SNR KAHLO is intrigued and warming to his task. FRIDA begins to enjoy her mother's compromise.)

KAHLO: She has given us much trouble. Her sexual inclinations are complex. Women as well as men, you understand?

S. KAHLO: Shut up, you old fool!

KAHLO: A man in your position cannot afford scandal.

DIEGO: I adore scandal.

S. KAHLO: He is a saint. (*She blesses herself.*)

KAHLO: Then, what of the expense?

S. KAHLO: (*out the window to the men*) He wants her! Let him have her for the love of the Virgin!

KAHLO: But, he has to know. Already, Frida's hospital treatment has brought me to bankruptcy. And she has suffered because we could not afford what she needs. She will always demand a great deal of your time and attention. (*to his wife*) He must know this.

(*DIEGO turns away, pricked by guilt. The scene fades as the lights return to the Park. FRIDA comes swiftly to his side.*)

SCENE SEVEN

FRIDA: What is the matter?

DIEGO: Just something your father said.

FRIDA: What? What did he say?

(*CATARINA summons her next scene to life. AN-GELINA BELOFF enters. She is a thin, pale, "bluebird" of a woman. She is DIEGO'S first wife. They are in their Paris studio. ANGELINA wipes a child's brow. She realises, as DIEGO has done, that the child has taken a turn for the worse. [The child may be an imaginary figure.]*)

DIEGO: Angelina? Angelina?

FRIDA: Don't go away.

DIEGO: The child!

SCENE EIGHT

FRIDA: Come back to the Park. (*FRIDA'S bed is brought on.*) Always leaving. Some nights I'd sit close by and watch you fade into some distant sadness. Where did you go? Back to Paris? To Angelina?

176

To see again the meningitis rise in a fever to smother your son, the little Diego. We shared a secret he and I, across the sea I lay besieged by polio and held his hand across the borderline.

(*CATARINA takes FRIDA'S hand and leads her to her bed. FRIDA'S parents stand vigil by her side. FRIDA is suffering from polio. She is aged six. ANGELINA begins to break down in despair and frustration.*)

DIEGO: I'll go for a doctor.

ANGELINA: Don't run away. (*She picks the boy up and cuddles him, whispering into his ear softly and urgently.*) Now, now, come now, my little Diego, come now. Listen to me, baby, listen. You must not go away, you must fight to stay with us, hmm? You must not go away. (*ANGELINA hums a tune.*)

S.KAHLO: She is on fire. The little thing, she will not last the night. I knew, I always knew that she could break my heart.

KAHLO: She is fighting very hard.

(*SENORA KAHLO hums a tune to FRIDA. ANGELINA looks at DIEGO.*)

DIEGO: What do you want me to do? Anything, I'll do anything for you, Angelina. What could I have done? Eh? Should I have signed up and paid you a soldier's wages, joined their slaughter? It's not my fault. I have done what I can, there's a war on. Nobody gives a damn about Cubism!

ANGELINA: Cubism? If he dies, Diego, you will have given me nothing. What will I have, eh? What will I have of you to show, to love and hold? You will leave me. You'll leave me now, you bastard, won't you? Nothing to stay for. I suppose you'll run back to Marievna and her brat. That's probably where you would have gone now. Can't you do something? Can't you do something? Anything! Go out and rob somebody, you could have stolen the medicine. Go out and murder for him. All you do is paint. (*She picks up a tube of paint.*) Eat it! Eat it!

(*DIEGO stops her. The song ends. For the RIVERAS this means their child is dead.*)

KAHLO: It has passed.

S.KAHLO: Sleeping. (*They are relieved.*)

ANGELINA: Oh my God, oh my God, breathe into him, breathe into him. Diego!

DIEGO: (*He is deeply distressed and holds her.*) He is gone. Let him go. What have I done? Angelina, help me. What have I done?

(*CATARINA steals the child's spirit and cradles it in her arms.*)

ANGELINA: So beautiful, a beautiful thing, he wanted you so much.

(*She tries to touch his face. He turns away.*)

DIEGO: Frida?! (*He turns towards her, the sick child, for comfort. ANGELINA exits, rejected by him. FRIDA turns towards him. They hold one another with a sense of great need. Lights return to the Park.*)

SCENE NINE

DIEGO: I looked after you, didn't I?

FRIDA: I wanted to fly but only ever got straw wings.

DIEGO: What will I do without my Friducita? When my son died, I looked at life, at the World War, then I looked at my painting. What was I doing? Millions dead and there I was painting Cubist still lives of pipes and violins. The world was crying out for an explanation and I sat in cafés arguing with Picasso about the problems of space on a flat surface!

FRIDA: From death comes life. You learnt how to listen.

DIEGO: Even here in the Park
If one treads carefully
The motion of the earth can be felt
Its process is heard in the humming of the stones
Felt in the soil, rich with our blood.
Its richness is sucked.
If one listens one can hear the sucking
Up into the veins of plants.
Always, always trying to reach the sun!
The role of Art is to describe the social revolution.
Man in his context.
The Fecund Earth!

FRIDA: This is why I married you. Don't let that die with me.

DIEGO: Isn't it the most beautiful feeling in the world, to be wanted?

(*They kiss.*)

SCENE TEN

(*CATARINA signals and CALAVERAS enter in dance bringing on an overweight dove holding a ribbon banner [see Frida's 1931 portrait] which is held above the couple. The ribbon is inscribed "Here you see us on our wedding day, me Frida Kahlo with my beloved husband, Diego Rivera". FRIDA arranges DIEGO and herself for the portrait. The CALAVERAS are dressed*)

179

as guests from FRIDA and DIEGO'S wedding party.)

DIEGO: You are Mexico, and when I die I will lie in you forever.

FRIDA: Makes a change from lying to me.

DIEGO: I would never betray you.

FRIDA: See what I mean.

(They laugh.)

FRIDA: *(to audience and guests)* Frida and Diego as Mexicanista Folk Art! *(to DIEGO)* I hope you think it is a good likeness.

DIEGO: You know, you have the face of a dog.

FRIDA: I suffered two grave accidents in my life, the second of which was Diego Rivera. And you have the face of a fat frog.

(LUPE MARIN, DIEGO'S second wife, has arrived late to the party. She puts her hands over DIEGO'S eyes. The scene freezes. LUPE is an elegant, cultured woman of a fiery and jealous disposition.)

DIEGO: Who is that?

FRIDA: Don't you remember? Lupe Marin. You invited her to our wedding party.

DIEGO: Ay, ay, ay. I'm sorry, it was just a bit of fun.

FRIDA: Too late now. It happened.

(The party comes to life.)

FRIDA: It was very good of you to come, Lupe. Can I....

LUPE: Not at all, Frida. It was very generous of you. Besides, I didn't want to ruin your fun. People will be most impressed by you, having his wife at your wedding. You should have brought Angelina over from Paris, Diego, then you could have had all three of us in one room. She is still in

Paris, isn't she? Still waiting for you to send for her? Get me a drink, dear. I have been running after Diego's children all day, I'm exhausted.

(*LUPE freezes. She is hard, proud and hurt.*)

FRIDA: (*to audience*) Lupe has a way with words.

(*The party comes to life.*)

DIEGO: I've read the latest draft of your novel.

LUPE: And?

DIEGO: Scurrilous, defamatory and wonderfully entertaining.

LUPE: Oh, Diego. (*She misses him and freezes in a plea.*)

DIEGO: (*to FRIDA*) I should have known she would do something.

FRIDA: You did know, that was why you invited her.

(*Party resumes as DIEGO relishes kissing LUPE in front of FRIDA.*)

DIEGO: How is life with your new husband, Lupe?

LUPE: Unbelievably happy. Give me more money for the children.

SIQUEIROS: Frida, one word, excuse us.

(*LUPE freezes again.*)

FRIDA: Siqueiros saved me from her.

DIEGO: A great painter, a lousy sense of loyalty.

(*The party resumes as FRIDA kisses SIQUEIROS in front of DIEGO.*)

FRIDA: Thank you. (*to SIQUEIROS*)

SIQUEIROS: Frida, you have been a good friend, a comrade but you should know that trouble is coming. Your friends over there, Bert and Ella Wolfe, they have broken with Stalin.

181

FRIDA: I know but....

SIQUEIROS: Diego is heading for trouble.

FRIDA: Why?

SIQUEIROS: He is too influenced by them. Stalin has told us to mount an insurrection. Diego is opposing it. There is no room for posturing.

FRIDA: Perhaps Diego knows what is best for Mexico, not someone in Russia.

SIQUEIROS: I will not shoot Diego or you, but don't be surprised if someone does.

(FRIDA moves back to DIEGO. The party freezes.)

FRIDA: We were so lucky, so lucky.

DIEGO: So were they.

(The party resumes.)

FRIDA: My darling Ella.

DIEGO: Bert, are you leaving already?

BERT: I can't believe that you invited Siqueiros.

FRIDA: He is a great Artist and comrade.

ELLA: That man has more blood on his hands than paint.

BERT: A little more and he might get a Lenin Peace prize.

FRIDA: Diego?

ELLA: We escape Moscow to find the same things happening here.

BERT: We'd better go. I don't want to be the cause of an embarrassing scene and get shot at your wedding.

ELLA: Isn't that what you wanted, Diego? Why else invite both camps?

DIEGO: I look after my friends. You are safe here. It is a clear message to others not to harm you.

(*LUPE has been drinking.*)

LUPE: Well, come on everybody, let's not overstay our welcome. No doubt Diego wants to be alone with his little Mexicanista wife. (*LUPE lifts up FRI-DA'S dress to reveal her deformed right leg.*) Look at these two sticks. These are the legs Diego has now, instead of mine!

(*LUPE turns to leave.*)

SCENE ELEVEN

(*The Park.*)

DIEGO: Frida?

FRIDA: Always playing with people's lives!

(*CATARINA takes FRIDA'S hand.*)

DIEGO: I'm sorry. Please. Where are you going?

CATARINA: Nothing out of the ordinary. Just getting on a bus.

DIEGO: No, Frida, don't go there. Let us walk in the Park.

SCENE TWELVE

(*The CALAVERAS form FRIDA'S painting 'The Bus'.*)

DIEGO: Frida, don't get on the bus with Alejandro, not today.

ALEJANDRO:(*FRIDA'S first serious lover, a gentle intellectual.*)

Come on, Frida, I will be late, my mother will get suspicious!

DIEGO: Don't go with him, please?

FRIDA: Tell her you left your books on the bus.

ALEJANDRO: I don't forget things. Not like you. You take care of nothing.

FRIDA: But I love my little parasol.

ALEJANDRO: Then why leave it everywhere we go! It seems you are careless with everything you love. (*FRIDA starts to "cry". ALEJANDRO becomes embarrassed.*) Stop it. (*People are looking.*) People think I have abused you. If you don't stop, I am getting off.

FRIDA: (*Stops "crying" instantly.*) This isn't about my parasol. You just want to punish me.

ALEJANDRO: Why shouldn't I? It is a scandal. Everyone is talking.

FRIDA: I am not ashamed.

ALEJANDRO: No, oh no, you can go with students, lecturers, caretakers behind my back, that is nothing to be ashamed of is it? Now, now you go with a woman... in the public library!

FRIDA: Ssh.

ALEJANDRO: I thought you weren't ashamed?

FRIDA: I didn't mean it to... it was an accident.

ALEJANDRO: An accident?

FRIDA: Yes.

ALEJANDRO: Oh, well at least that makes me feel better.

FRIDA: It does?

ALEJANDRO: Why, of course. Now when people gossip I can say, "No, you have it all wrong. It was an accident. Frida tripped on a book and went head first up another woman's skirt!"

FRIDA: Not that kind of accident!

(*A "CHILD" CALAVERA on the bus cries out as CATARINA pantomimes the reactions of the tram driver who is about to crash into the bus.*)

CHILD: Look mummy, that tram.

FRIDA: Hey, look out! (*to DRIVER of bus*)

ALEJANDRO: What is the driver dong? Hey! Mind out! That tram!

FRIDA: Slow down!

ALEJANDRO: Stop!

(*ALEJANDRO steps from the image of frozen impact.*)

ALEJANDRO: A tramcar came around a corner. Our bus driver seemed to freeze. He did nothing, just sat in terror, we all did, just sat for an eternity. The bus bowed under the force of the tramcar, then seemed to explode. Frida's clothes were torn from her.... The medical report listed her injuries. Her right leg broken in eleven places. Her right foot crushed. One collar bone was fractured and her left shoulder dislocated. She had two broken ribs and broke her spine and pelvis in three places each. A metal handrail had broken away and she had become impaled upon it. It passed through her abdomen and came out through her vagina.

(*CATARINA takes FRIDA from the image and spins her slowly like a musical box ballerina.*)

A man sitting next to us was on his way to the theatre. He was carrying a tin of golden glitter for some special effect or other, which exploded, showering her with its contents. When I crawled out of the wreckage I saw her, still standing, bewildered, searching for her parasol. A huge crowd gathered and stared in amazement as she teetered about. "La Ballerina!" they cried, "See, it is a ballerina."

SCENE THIRTEEN

(*Lights up on the Park as CATARINA holds FRIDA in her arms.*)

FRIDA: So, I lost my virginity! They promised me I could fly but I only ever got straw wings.

DIEGO: It killed you, that crash. Twenty-nine years later, but that was it. We would have had longer together. I wouldn't be a stupid old man, sitting alone, talking to himself in the park.

FRIDA: Everyone seemed crazy to me after the crash, all searching for something. But I knew then what we have is life. We already have it. And I loved it. "A wonderful investigation of space." Hey, without the accident, I would never have sat still long enough to paint. Maybe this way I have been a little use in this world, eh? Do you think?

DIEGO: Without Art I cannot see how we can ever wholly know the world.

FRIDA: Without Art we cannot know ourselves.

DIEGO: You are right.

FRIDA: And so were you. You painted yourself in the Alameda Park.

DIEGO: Myself in the world, the world in me. You taught me that. Thank you.

SCENE FOURTEEN

> (*FRIDA and DIEGO kiss. The CALAVERAS dance on dressed as the INDIAN FAMILY and the POLICEMAN from the 'Alameda Park' mural. At the end of the dance they freeze in a depiction of the mural.*)

DIEGO: And here, as a boy, here in the Park, I watched an Indian family.

> (*An INDIAN FAMILY are being pushed out of the Park by a POLICEMAN.*)

POLICEMAN: Get out. Keep moving. You know you're not allowed in the Parks.

> (*The INDIANS are not aggressive. They know the situation.*)

IND. WMN: Don't push me.

IND. MAN: Leave her.

POLICEMAN: Well, get moving.

IND. MAN: This is my country!

IND. BOY: Leave my dad alone, you.

POLICEMAN: Move.

IND. MAN: I said, don't push her.

POLICEMAN: You know you people don't do yourselves any favours, do you? What would it be like if they ever let you in? You're your own worst enemies. Now out!

> (*They freeze as the mural once again. DIEGO paints them as if they are the mural.*)

DIEGO: Now we are all free to walk in the Park.

IND. MAN: Even the beggars.

IND. WMN: Yes, it's a great country now you are free to be a beggar in the Park. (*to POLICEMAN*) When Zapata rises we will rise with him.

IND. MAN: But this time we will not be fooled. We will take back our common lands and live in the good old ways of our ancestors.

IND. WMN: And we will have cars and tractors! And if you try to stop us we will kill you and your children! What are you doing? (*to DIEGO*)

DIEGO: I am painting you. Here, take a look.

(*INDIAN WOMAN steps out of painting to look at it.*)

IND. WMN: Ha! It's good. Hey, look at him! (*the POLICEMAN*) Yes, Senor Painter, that is how it is. Oh, my goodness! Enrique, you look....

IND. MAN: What? I'm supposed to be angry. (*referring to his expression in the painting*)

IND. WMN: It's so funny. Ah! (*She kisses her son who grimaces and wipes his face.*) Why paint us, we are just Indians?

(*She goes back into the painting.*)

DIEGO: Can you read?

IND. MAN: No.

DIEGO: So, I paint.

(*The depiction is reformed.*)

DIEGO: I want to create discussion on street corners.

(*The CALAVERAS break into another dance. They chase the POLICEMAN away.*)

SCENE FIFTEEN

(A street café. The POLICEMAN returns with a SOLDIER. They have guns. CATARINA parodies them.)

DIEGO: You were a child of that revolution.

POLICEMAN: Hey you, Diego Rivera! You know what you are? A traitor! Well, we've had enough. Long live the Mexican Army! *(He pulls a gun.)*

FRIDA: Oh my God, I remember this.

DIEGO: Frida.

FRIDA: No! Stop! *(She stands in front of DIEGO.)* If you fucking sons of bitches want to kill him you shoot me first! You hear me!

SOLDIER: There's no need for language.

POLICEMAN: *(to SOLDIER)* Shut up! *(to FRIDA)* Out of the way!

FRIDA: Where are you from, eh? Little Mexican boys? Do you know who you are killing? This man fights for your mother and father to live better lives! Get out of the way! You shits! You gun down great men like cowards. Shoo, shoo. Or do you kill unarmed women as well?! How brave are you? Shoot me?

INDIANS: Hey! Hey! What's going on? Leave them! *(etc.)*

(The assassins have lost the moment and run. FRIDA collapses into DIEGO.)

FRIDA: They could have taken you.

DIEGO: Thank God. Thank God, Frida that you learnt to fight so hard for life.

FRIDA: We were everyone's favourite traitors. Siqueiros had his say, too.

SCENE SIXTEEN

(*A meeting of communists and workers.*)

SIQUEIROS: Comrades, the time has come to recognise that Rivera has degenerated into a lackey of the rich. He takes money from the American Ambassador.

FRIDA: To paint a revolutionary mural!

(*DIEGO indicates that FRIDA should not react.*)

SIQUEIROS: Whilst every other painter in Mexico has been thrown out of work by the government of assassins, Rivera is still employed by them.

FRIDA: But look what he is painting! The history of Mexico!

SIQUIEROS: He paints history because he cannot face the future. His latest efforts are whimsical depictions of an idealised past. No wonder the gringos love them. And now we hear that Rivera has been invited to paint in the USA and do you know who he will paint for? The San Francisco Stock Exchange Club, Edsel Ford and John D. Rockefeller Junior! Actions speak louder than words. Know Rivera by his actions.

(*DIEGO takes the stand.*)

DIEGO: From myth we interpret our future! Perhaps you would rather destroy Mexican culture like Stalin has the Russian. Destroy history so that we no longer know who we are. Then perhaps we would be foolish enough to agree with Stalin. Stalin, who sends orders to the Mexican Communist Party, run by painters, to mount an armed insurrection. The few thousand they were able to muster were slaughtered or imprisoned. Now, because I argued against the insurrection I am somehow responsible for it failing. Like Trotsky, I am blamed for the failure of Stalinism.

(*SIQUEIROS draws a gun.*)

SIQUEIROS: You coward! You hide behind Trotsky because you cannot accept discipline. You are a bourgeois individualist! (*SIQUEIROS fires into the air.*) Long live Stalin, death to all social democrats!

DIEGO: (*drawing a gun and firing also*) Long live Trotsky, death to fascism and capitalism!

(*ACTORS run for cover. SIQUEIROS and DIEGO come face to face. It is suddenly rather embarrassing.*)

SIQUEIROS: We'd better get out of here. Go with Trotsky, Diego and you will force us to kill you.

DIEGO: Siqueiros, all this, all these political slogans are not big enough to hide the fact that you know I'm a better painter than you are.

SIQUEIROS: You oaf, do you really think that there is so little at stake?

(*SIQUEIROS freezes.*)

FRIDA: Ay, ay, ay, Diego. (*admonishing*)

DIEGO: Which way now?

SCENE SEVENTEEN

(*Lights return to the Park.*)

FRIDA: The only way that was left open to us. Accept the commissions in Gringolandia. I would never go along with it now. Trotskyism is an irrelevance, an intellectual ghetto. The real power is in the Party. (*she indicates SIQUEIROS*) We were foolish to leave it.

DIEGO: Now you are so self-righteous, but then? You just
                wanted to see the world.

FRIDA: I could have done without seeing Detroit.

SCENE EIGHTEEN

(*The CALAVERAS come to life as morbid city workers
as a US style song is performed. They become
WORKERS in a biological warfare factory and a
NURSE and DOCTOR. These characters come from
DIEGO'S Detroit mural. The main singer is a FORD
WORKER.*)

Buying time
I'll always be buying time
Wishing away the hours
I'm selling to the masters of time
Mr J. P. Morgan and Mr Henry Ford
J.D. Rockefeller and the rest of the board.
They know just where to find me
I'm in the line for bread.
I sell my time for living
Buying time to be dead.
Buying time
I guess they'll always be buying time.
And I'm wishing away the hours
Till I can buy a moment that is mine.

DIEGO: I shall paint the machine age.
                The modern era.
                Man and machine.
                The collective heroes.
                My paint will prize the revolution out of the
                                              Depression.

(Depiction of DIEGO'S Detroit mural, 'The North Wall'. A DOCTOR and a NURSE on stage left, are surrounded by a HORSE, a SHEEP and a COW. Two gas-masked figures make a bomb on stage right. They represent the use and misuse of science. The DOCTOR is innoculating a child. DIEGO picks up his brush and palette.)

DIEGO: From the phials of scientists pours Life or death.

SCIEN. 1: How're we doing?

SCIEN. 2: Fine. That's two parts black-death to three parts leprosy. Now we need one-part motor-neuron disease.

SCIEN. 1: Check. Where's this aimed for?

SCIEN. 2: Leningrad. Check.

FRIDA: Diego, the Communist Party has denounced the murals as a glorification of capitalism. They do not intend to defend you.

DIEGO: Ah, Stalin. Now he supports censorship in the USA as well.

FRIDA: What are you going to do?

DIEGO: Paint.

(FRIDA is frustrated by DIEGO.)

SCIEN. 1: Hey, what's he painting us for? What's going on?

SCIEN. 1: Goddamn it. What if Mary and the kids see?

SCIEN. 2: We've got to get this stopped.

SCIEN. 1: You're right. Mary?!

(The CAST begin making farmyard noises.)

NURSE: Hi, honey. Got any new drugs to help this child?

SCIEN. 1: Erm.... We're working on it.

NURSE: Don't forget it's little Bobby's birthday today.

ALL: Don't you just love children?

SCIEN. 2:   Mary, Rivera, he's painted you surrounded by farmyard animals!

DOCTOR: Yeah, I wondered about that. I thought we were meant to be in a hospital.

SCIEN. 1:   Don't you see? It's blasphemous.

NURSE: What? Oh my goodness, of course! He's made it look like the stable at Bethlehem.

DOCTOR: You mean this is Christ? (*the baby*) Hey, that's smart.

NURSE: Smart? Dr Joseph, if we are innoculating Christ then he can't be immortal, can he?

DOCTOR: I guess not.

SCIEN. 1:   You tell him, Mary! This painting is a crime against God and all that's decent in America.

DOCTOR: But surely he has the right to his opinion?

SCIEN. 2:   Doctor, take a look at what he's painted below us. The Ford Factory. Who wants to come to an Art gallery and see workers making cars?

FORD
WORKER: Hey, wait a minute.

DOCTOR: Yes, I see, it is an architectural disaster. It completely destroys the Louis XIV style foyer area.

SCIEN. 2:   It's got to be destroyed!

DOCTOR: But, I mean, destroying Art... isn't that a mite intolerant?

MARY: Doctor, listen to the way we're speaking. Don't you think this is becoming a little didactic?

DOCTOR: Didactic? Yes, I feel distinctly didactic.

ALL: Oh, my God, we're all becoming didactic!

DOCTOR: Okay, guys. Let's destroy it.

(*They freeze in vicious poses.*)

FORD
WORKER: Mr Rivera, we've just had a meeting up at Ford. Eight thousand Ford workers have agreed to mount a picket to protect a mural.

DIEGO: Eight thousand?

FRIDA: Thank you, thank you very much.

SCIEN. 2: Eight thousand.

DOCTOR: Eight thousand standing outside?

MARY: This is intimidation!

DIEGO: Now let's see them attack us. Innoculate my child.

FORD
WORKER: Do as he says.

(*They do so by reforming the depiction.*)

DIEGO: This is my gift to Angelina.

(*FRIDA is hurt. She goes towards the baby Jesus.*)

SCENE NINETEEN

(*Lights return to the Park as the depiction breaks up. CATARINA steals the baby Jesus then acts in a panic as if the baby has stopped breathing. She shakes the baby violently but comically, then weeps. As she exits, CATARINA laughs at FRIDA.*)

DIEGO: Frida?

FRIDA: Don't touch me! (*DIEGO tries to speak.*) I don't want to talk to you. I want to talk to Doctor Eloesser! My doctorcito.

SCENE TWENTY

(Lights up on ELOESSER. As in FRIDA'S portrait of him, he carries a model boat.)

ELOESSER: I showed your x-rays to my students the other day. They diagnosed you were dead already.

(FRIDA laughs.)

FRIDA: What can I do with him? I am a widow to his painting. Eighteen, twenty hours a day, but that I can live with, just. No, I can't. I want him to paint but he widows me over and over with these other women. It kills me.

ELOESSER: You must stay calm. Any tension aggravates your injuries.

FRIDA: I caught him at it. Well, not at it, but... I could see he adored her.

ELOESSER: Who?

FRIDA: Helen Wills-Moody.

ELOESSER: The tennis champion? Are you sure Diego could go a game, set and match with an athlete?

FRIDA: Him, no. His penis, yes. That thing does press-ups every morning. I can never possess him, even when he is inside me he is in the process of leaving.

SCENE TWENTY-ONE

(HELEN WILLS-MOODY enters. DIEGO sketches her. FRIDA enters the scene. Lights change.)

196

FRIDA: Diego! Where have you been? Three days. Why didn't you tell me where you were?

DIEGO: It just happened that way.

FRIDA: Rubbish. Everyone knew where you were, except me. They are too embarrassed to tell me.

DIEGO: Helen, meet Frida, my wife.

HELEN: Hello. My goodness, you really do look like they say.

FRIDA: And so do you cuate, a Californian to your teeth.

            (*FRIDA smiles.*)

HELEN: I guess so. I'd better practice.

            (*HELEN takes up her posture from the painting.*)

FRIDA: So, you have been working at your tennis for the last three days?

DIEGO: Helen will be my centre piece, my California, in the Stock Exchange Mural. Women here are so much freer. She is a marvellous creature, strong, independent, healthy and maternal. She will mirror my portrait of Lupe at Chapingo, a mother earth, a bountiful provider.

FRIDA: Does she know this?

DIEGO: Of course.

FRIDA: You usually discuss with me first.

DIEGO: I am sorry. (*lying*) It was to be a surprise.

FRIDA: I think it's a mistake. Your female California should be a Mexican. This land was stolen from us. If we still had it perhaps Mexican children would grow as strong as her. Maybe then we could fuck like she does!

DIEGO: Is there anything that you want? I have work to do.

SCENE TWENTY-TWO

(Lights up on DR ELOESSER. This scene is continuous from scene twenty.)

FRIDA: He is a grown man. Perhaps I am still a child. I was unfaithful to Alejandro. Why am I a hypocrite? I don't want to own him. How could I own a genius? I just... I want more sex. I want to know if I can have a child. Can I carry one to full term?

ELOESSER: Are you pregnant? *(She is.)* Does Diego know? *(He doesn't.)* If you lie still and I mean still, you might make it. It will probably mean a caesarean. Your pelvis is held together by faith. The weight of a child, well, you risk your own life. Is this going to answer any of your needs?

FRIDA: Yes, yes, of course.

ELOESSER: I mean is it going to change Diego?

FRIDA: I want him inside me. I want him to play with, to love me without reservation.

ELOESSER: How will you paint and look after a child?

FRIDA: I know, I know.

(DIEGO enters the scene. He is furious.)

DIEGO: Tell her I forbid it. I have had all the children I need. If I am lucky, I have fifteen years left. All I want to do is paint. I have never lied. I want to paint! I have always said that.

FRIDA: Oh, so because you've always said that it's all right?

ELOESSER: Hey, hey hey. Calm down.

DIEGO: If you want children, go ahead, but you have them in Mexico. I stay here. Go home to your mother!

(They storm apart into separate lights. DIEGO is suddenly panicked.)

SCENE TWENTY-THREE

DIEGO: Frida? *(anxiously)*

FRIDA: What?

DIEGO: I thought you had gone for a moment.

FRIDA: Images, images, what should I do? *(Depiction of 'On the Border Line'.)* Frida Kahlo on the borderline between Mexico and the United States. The land of ancient reason or the land of machine greed. Who wants children? I have a good life. I can travel, be with Diego, meet people, get drunk, sleep late, paint, get dressed in my own time, pack my own bag and travel light. Children.

On the borderline.

I love being pregnant. I feel sassy and bold, full and fertile, strong. I want to bump people out of my way with my stomach. Hey, mind out, Frida's coming through! I want to stroke my face along his body. I will wash his little genitals and when no one is watching, I will put them in my mouth and make him giggle.

On the borderline.

(She breaks the depiction.)

FRIDA: Doctorcito, cut off my head.

ELOESSER: Your head?

FRIDA: Then I will only do what my body wants. This portrait I paint for you.

(*During scene twenty-four, FRIDA becomes CHRIST, then an AZTEC human sacrifice, then CHRIST again. CALAVERAS transform similarly, acting out the rituals.*)

SCENE TWENTY-FOUR

FRIDA: (*CHRISTIAN section with humour and relish.*) My mother would take us to the nearby church. Cast into darkness and the icy touch of dead skin, our eyes would adjust and from the gloom came Christ, a bloody, tortured creature bowed beneath his cross to bear, a fragile spine to snap. (*AZTEC section. CATARINA plunges a knife into FRIDA.*) (*CHRISTIAN section.*) His flesh peels in tatters from the whip and drips with copious blood. One can see inside the wounds, to exposed bone and tissue. His head studded with thorns pours blood into eyes which trickles to describe the starved outline of his jaw. (*A crown of thorns is placed around FRIDA'S neck.*) His eyes, a frozen plea of anguish. Why, why, didn't you try to save me? (*She is left alone and weak. DIEGO goes to her aid. DR ELOESSER smiles knowingly at them.*) And so he holds us in his grip. (*FRIDA smiles at the audience. DIEGO does not see. DIEGO gives way.*)

DIEGO: You must look after it. Don't expect any help from me. This is your decision. I will not stand in your way.

FRIDA: It is a boy. I know it. A little Dieguieto. Don't be jealous.

           (*CATARINA leads the CALAVERAS around FRIDA.*)

DIEGO: What? What is she doing here?

FRIDA: Please don't take me, please!

DIEGO: Where are you going?!

CATARINA: You cannot forget the bus, you must not.

FRIDA: No, please, don't take my baby.

(*The CALAVERAS take FRIDA. They coo and giggle, rocking her.*)

DIEGO: Dimly in a hotel bedroom
Life flickered.
Street lights cast a glow
Through screams laid thick upon the air
Illuminating in their misery
The blood of son and mother.

FRIDA: What war did I ever ask for?
Spewing blood onto a cotton palette
Miscarried matter
My little Dieguieto
Disintegrated in the womb
What war did I ever ask for?
Here justice was miscarried.
Surely?

(*FRIDA and the CALAVERAS act out the contractions, a jerking violent dance.*)

DIEGO: She lay in terror like a child
Waking in the night
Her slender thighs I've kissed and parted
Smeared with unctious corpuscles
Congealed and overlaid afresh
With bloody matter.
Repulsion?
Yes.

CATARINA: For her, left nothing.
A dream flushed out that night.
No product for the pain.
No bubbling babe.
No warm congratulation.
No embrace or flowers.

CALAVERAS: No "good girl, well done."

(CATARINA is summoning the child from FRIDA'S womb.)

DIEGO: I've watched her when her period comes
Look to the blood in some relief
Then cry aloud inside her room
For another lost companion.
I cannot pretend to understand.
I can hear but I cannot listen.
Until she paints, I see but I am not perceiving.
From that death came Frida's life
In painting, painting, painting.

(A depiction of 'My Birth' by FRIDA.)

(End of ACT ONE.)

Act Two

SCENE TWENTY-FIVE

(*Lights up on DIEGO and his ASSISTANTS with FRIDA. They strike a depiction of the 'Rockefeller Mural'. A MAN stands in the middle, the MILITARY to the right, WORKERS to the left. They sing.*)

Man looking to the future
Hope and high vision
Man as the centre of the universe
Geared for transmission.
Modern man
Pulling at the levers in the war with nature
Who controls the modern plan
Controls our future
Modern man.

(*The depiction breaks down. FRIDA sits down and watches DIEGO and his ASSISTANTS. They are at work on the Rockefeller Mural. They are grinding colours, testing them, plastering the wall and marking out the painting containing Lenin's portrait. An ASSISTANT is tracing the drawing onto the plaster by piercing the drawing. All activity can be mimed. The painting need not be represented at all. BERT and ELLA WOLFE are with FRIDA.*)

ELLA: He's walked right into a trap.

FRIDA: Diego believes that Rockefeller will keep his word.

ELLA: Taking money from Rockefeller! The communists

203

are having a field day.

BERT: Ella, give it a rest.

ELLA: No, they can denounce us as friends of Diego. We all become soiled by the money. If he wants to paint then come to the New York Workers School with us and paint for the unemployed.

BERT: What's he supposed to live on? Air? He's no different from Michelangelo, a homosexual painting for the Catholic Church, I don't suppose he felt completely uncompromised either. It's his living.

ELLA: But what if Rockefeller continues to insist that the portrait of Lenin be removed? Then what does he do? Give in? What's more important to Diego, his ambition or his responsibility as an artist?

BERT: Ella, you are out of line. Diego has never shown anything but integrity.

ELLA: Except to his wife, of course.

FRIDA: What do you mean?

ELLA: Nothing, nothing. I'm sorry.

FRIDA: Tell me.

BERT: Now who's compromised, Ella?

(*We hear the pounding of SOLDIERS' feet. CATARINA enters, parodying the troops with their guns. These are Rockefeller's POLICE, sent to stop the painters.*)

DIEGO: What do you want? What do you want, eh? Talk to them in English, what do they want? Why the guns?

STEPHEN: They say we must stop painting right now, Maestro, get off the scaffold.

LUCIENNE: What are we going to do? Maestro?

DIEGO: I made a deal with Rockefeller! I told him I would balance the portrait of Lenin with those of John Brown and Abraham Lincoln.

(*ELLA scoffs at DIEGO. FRIDA is angry. She yells at the troops.*)

FRIDA: (*to GUARDS*) You cannot stop the painting. Not your guns, not your thugs. Tell Mr Rockefeller that he signed the contracts, approved the drafts, he cannot stop the painting!

DIEGO: Why doesn't Mr Rockefeller come to New York and see the work, talk to me?!

LUCIENNE: This is not just your painting any more, Diego. It belongs to all of us, everyone.

FLORES: And it isn't Rockefeller's either. If he buys the Sistine chapel he doesn't buy the right to destroy it.

STEPHEN: (*to GUARDS*) Give us a moment!

(*DIEGO looks up at the mural. He struggles with whether or not to remove it.*)

ARTHUR: Diego, if you remove the portrait of Lenin, we will not work for you. The painting is right the way it is.

(*DIEGO agrees.*)

STEPHEN: They say we must come down, Maestro.

DIEGO: Which way now?!

FRIDA: Diego, if you give way I'll never trust you again as long as I live!

(*Lights go down to focus upon CATARINA and DIEGO who both say the following speech:*)

SCENE TWENTY-SIX

DIEGO &
CATARINA: Here a moment is not an instant.
Isolated, lost, without cousins,
But a prism through which
All history can be focused
And cast upon a surface.

(The CALAVERAS recreate images from Diego's murals dipicting the story of the Spanish conquest.)

FRIDA: Remember Diego, remember and fight.

BERT: When the Spanish came to the valley of Mexico
The Aztec Lord Montezuma
Believed Cortes to be a man of honour
Believed he was the saviour Quetzalcoatl.

ELLA: Only Montezuma's general, Cauhtemoc, knew that this was not the work of Gods but of men, of conquerors! Cortez gathered an army against the city of Tenochitlan.

FRIDA: Too late, Cauhtemoc was defeated, our temples were destroyed, our murals and sculptures smashed. Is it going to happen to us again? *(to DIEGO)*

DIEGO: When Cortes conquered the valley of Mexico.

(The CALAVERAS sing Latin plainsong.)

The priest swept in his syphillitic shadow
Their skirts raising dust in flurries
Like busy women clearing up after a dictator's
                                        garden party.
Obscuring, obscuring, removing all trace.
Our culture erased
˙We are gone.
We cannot think
We cannot remember
We are beholden to Rockefeller for the truth.

CALAVERA:(*sings*) The good Lord Rockefeller.

> (*The CALAVERAS end depicting the mural 'Man at the Crossroads'.*)

SCENE TWENTY-SEVEN

STEPHEN: Maestro, please, they say we must come down or there'll be trouble.

DIEGO: Look at it! (*The mural.*) Look. Remember. It was a painting of hope for the future. A man was here.

ARTHUR: A worker.

DIEGO: He was looking up, with hope, a sort of.... He was at the controls of a machine which forms the centre of the atom. To the right... to the right.

LUCIENNE: The forces of militarism, fascist soldiers, and the decadent rich.

ARTHUR: But on the other side, its dialectical opposite, the solidarity needed for peace, for health, for co-operation. The question is, who controls the man? Who controls science?

FRIDA: Who controls?

ARTHUR: Technology.

STEPHEN: Who controls hearts and minds?

DIEGO: And here, here was....

STEPHEN: Maestro, please, they say we must stop now.

DIEGO: You should have seen it.

> (*The characters repeat what they hear being said by Rockefeller's POLICE.*)

LUCIENNE: Get your things, Mr Rivera.

ARTHUR: Here's the balance owing, Mr Rivera.

STEPHEN: All square now.

DIEGO: You should have seen it.
             You should have seen
             The City of Tenochitlan
             Before the conquerors came
             There stood the pyramids,
             Opposing.
             One of night and one of day.
             You should have seen it.

LUCIENNE: Go back to Mexico, Mr Rivera, your services are
             no longer required.

SCENE TWENTY-EIGHT

(*The CALAVERAS taunt DIEGO. The scene breaks
down as Mexican music indicates their return home.
DIEGO is demoralised and depressed. FRIDA lies on
her bed with CATARINA. CRISTINA KAHLO
enters.*)

CRISTINA: Frida? (*offstage*)

DIEGO: (*offstage*) She is asleep!

CRISTINA: Diego? (*entering*)

             (*DIEGO is cleaning paint brushes.*)

DIEGO: Your sister is sleeping sweetly.

             (*He kisses her hand.*)

CRISTINA: How is she?

DIEGO: There has been a lot of pain. I feel quite helpless.
             They will take her into hospital again but I do not
             trust them here. I am exhausted by it.

CRISTINA: Poor Diego.

DIEGO: She was very sorry you did not bring the children yesterday. She had waited all afternoon.

CRISTINA: Was that yesterday? I forgot. Where is she?

DIEGO: In her house.

CRISTINA: Of course. I can't get used to this, two houses. It is too modern.

DIEGO: It is too modern. (*he laughs*)

CRISTINA: Why are you laughing?

DIEGO: Cristina, would you let me paint you? I would be flattered.

CRISTINA: Why me?

DIEGO: You have no pretensions. I always wonder why I never married you, why I marry women who are restless, always struggling for something. You always seem unaffected, at peace, calm.

CRISTINA: Frida says I live in the ether.

DIEGO: Frida patronises you. You know your own mind.

CRISTINA: What is ether?

DIEGO: A gas. It makes you giddy, anaesthetised.

CRISTINA: I thought it was something like that. She always says it with a smile, as if I'm cute or sweet. It makes me angry.

DIEGO: You shouldn't let Frida patronise you. You hear me? You are as unique as any one of us and much more beautiful. You are, in a way, pure, uncluttered. I would like to paint that. Will you let me?

CRISTINA: You say such nice things.

DIEGO: I mean everything, everything that I said.

CRISTINA: I wish, one day I could have a man who spoke to me as you do instead of just, you know.... Frida doesn't know how lucky she is.

DIEGO: Frida is not bad to me.

CRISTINA: She is, Diego. You deserve better, always so kind and generous to people. She shouldn't sleep around the way she does. Not for you.

DIEGO: Sex is very difficult for her. She is in pain so often.

CRISTINA: But Diego, when she isn't in pain she is with someone else. It is bad of her. I'm sorry, it is disloyal of me but I can't help it. It must be very awkward for you.

DIEGO: Frida demands a great deal. (*CRISTINA kisses him.*) Will you hold me, Cristina, please. (*They kiss passionately as CATARINA gloats.*)

SCENE TWENTY-NINE

(*FRIDA is painting 'A Few Small Nips'.*)

FRIDA: Just a few small nips
Said the murderer at the trial.
She'd messed me around.
I don't understand.
I just knifed her a bit.
A few small nips.
I never thought she'd bleed that much.
You can't blame me for that.

(*DIEGO breaks from the scene with CRISTINA.*)

DIEGO: Are we going to spend another day like this?

FRIDA: I don't give a damn about the sluts, the tourists, the patrons, but why fuck my sister?

DIEGO: I do not fuck her, we make love.

FRIDA: I'm going to talk to her.

DIEGO: Why are you doing this to yourself?

FRIDA: I'm going to get her to stop.

DIEGO: She will not stop.

FRIDA: Oh, won't she?!

DIEGO: She's not in your shadow any more, that's what hurts, doesn't it... Sisters!

FRIDA: Don't.... (*She attacks him. They struggle and shout at each other. FRIDA falls to the floor.*)

DIEGO: You've only yourself to blame. I didn't want to come back to Mexico. I love her!

(*LUPE enters and rushes to FRIDA'S defence.*)

LUPE: Frida! What are you doing to her? Get out of here! Get out. You pig! Before I smash your skull in two!

(*DIEGO exits.*)

FRIDA: He's killing me! He's killing me, Lupe.

LUPE: Here, here. (*She helps FRIDA up.*) That coyote, dog breath, son of a bitch! Who is he screwing now? Eh? Some slut?

FRIDA: No.

LUPE: He isn't?

FRIDA: No.

LUPE: Oh! What's the matter with him then?

FRIDA: It's nothing.

LUPE: Frida, I was married to that pig. Don't tell me it's nothing. What's he done to you?

FRIDA: Nothing.

LUPE: So, be proud. (*pause*) Look, the truth is I know already.

FRIDA: What?

LUPE: That's why I came here.

FRIDA: What do you know?

LUPE: About Cristina. (*pause*) He did it to me as well. (*pause*) With my sister. I came home and found them.

FRIDA: What did you do?

LUPE: I kicked her around the house. When I'd had enough of that I threw her out and told her "If you ever step foot in Mexico City again, I'll kill you!" Then I kicked Diego all around the house. Smashed everything. It's the only way.

FRIDA: No. No, I'll not give him the satisfaction. Nor her. If they want to destroy me then let them.

LUPE: Huh! You expect too much. If you let them shit on you they will. They'll say they never realised you were hurting.

FRIDA: I'll know they are lying.

LUPE: So what? They won't admit it. Never. Especially not to themselves. Make them pay.

FRIDA: How?

LUPE: Screw his best friend.

FRIDA: No.

SIQUEIROS: (*SIQUEIROS calls from offstage.*) Frida? Can I come in?

LUPE: Better still, screw his worst enemy.

SIQUEIROS: Ah! Lupe.

LUPE: I'm just going, David. Frida is bored with me. You entertain her, eh? Frida, you be a bad girl.

Remember what Lupe told you. Smash everything.

(*LUPE kisses FRIDA then exits.*)

SIQUEIROS: Smash everything? What's she talking about?

FRIDA: She is fire. I am earth. Or maybe even air.

(*SIQUEIROS looks at FRIDA'S painting and is repulsed.*)

SIQUEIROS: My God! Why that?

FRIDA: It is a retablo, a woman and a saint, only the saint has murdered the women by inflicting tiny wounds. A few small nips, he said at his trial. I read it in a newspaper.

SIQUEIROS: But why that?

FRIDA: I feel for her. (*pause*) I hear you are going to Spain. How I envy you. I would go and fight. I would give anything.

SIQUEIROS: Give us one thing. Tell Diego to go back to President Cardenas and say he made a mistake. Don't let Mexico grant Trotsky asylum. Allow us Mexicans to hold our heads high in Spain.

(*FRIDA'S loyalties are stretched.*)

FRIDA: Mexico can be proud that it protects the free expression of ideas.

SIQUEIROS: Trotsky has no hiding place. Stalin has passed the death sentence. It is only a matter of time. Free expression of ideas! Trotsky's supporters are undermining the Soviet Union and you....

FRIDA: Undermining Stalin, you mean.

SIQUEIROS: No, the Soviet Union. They must be stopped. The Party is more important than individuals.

FRIDA: Yes, yes, but truth is more important than obedience. The fact is that when Rockefeller destroyed Diego's mural your lot stayed silent. It's the same with the Soviet Union, all criticism, all poetry censored in favour of glorifying Stalin.

(*SIQUEIROS now feels compromised.*)

SIQUEIROS: Our task is to liberate the working people. That is more important than artistic freedom, surely?

FRIDA: When the people are liberating themselves the artist is freed. But look at any country repressing the working people and you will see grants withdrawn, universities closed, censorship! Tell me this is not happening.

SIQUEIROS: Frida, I respect your loyalty to your husband.

(*He makes to leave.*)

FRIDA: What do you mean by that?!

SIQUEIROS: Tell me, in your painting is the woman you or Mexico? I know the man is Diego.

FRIDA: When you go to Spain, take your brushes. The revolution needs painters.

(*FRIDA hands him a paint brush.*)

SIQUEIROS: No, Frida, in the end revolution demands pragmatism. It isn't an artistic debate. (*He hands her the paint brush.*) I'll take a gun.

(*She hugs him.*)

FRIDA: Be careful, Senor Siqueiros. I will do whatever I can.

(*They kiss goodbye.*)

SCENE THIRTY

(*Return to the Park.*)

FRIDA: (*to DIEGO*) I sold my first four paintings to Edward G. Robinson and gave Siqueiros the money.

DIEGO: (*sighs*) Perhaps I am an anarchist.

FRIDA: Diego, you can't just fool around with these words! These words could cost people their lives, damn it. They nearly killed us! You were a fool to bring that old Trotsky here.

SCENE THIRTY-ONE

(*NATALIA and LEON TROTSKY appear. She is very nervous. The stage becomes the Blue House and garden.*)

NATALIA: Is it safe?

FRIDA: All clear. Well, Natalia, welcome to the land of tortillas.

(*She serves them tequilla.*)

NATALIA: What is she saying?

FRIDA: What is she saying?

LEON: Nothing, no matter. Can we look around?

FRIDA: Salud. (*they drink*) Tequilla! The house is yours to loan. This is my family home. My father has vacated it for you.

LEON: Can we look around? (*they do so*)

NATALIA: At least it is cool in here.

LEON: This is marvellous, we can hold my trial in this room.

FRIDA: Your trial?

LEON: I am going to answer Stalin's charges against me. I intend to expose him. Whose is this painting?

FRIDA: Oh, it is one of mine. I will move it.

LEON: You painted this?

FRIDA: A long time ago.

LEON: I would love to see more. It is very affective.

FRIDA: Wait until you see Diego's murals. Here is the garden. If we ever feel besieged by doubts or demoralised, Diego's paintings fill us with pride and conviction.

LEON: Come, Nata. Nata, a garden! Oh, this is splendid, a garden!

NATALIA: What are these plants?

FRIDA: Cactus, we make Pulque from it. I will show you around.

NATALIA: Look! A monkey!

FRIDA: Yes. These are Calla lilies, Diego's favourite. They remind me of coitus, don't they you?

LEON: Yes, a little bit.

FRIDA: Ah well, a little bit of coitus is better than none at all.

(*TROTSKY laughs.*)

NATALIA: Perhaps you could show us the garden later?

(*The lights fade on the TROTSKYS.*)

SCENE THIRTY-TWO

DIEGO: Look at him, the old goat, already he is in love with you.

(*DIEGO loads his gun. We return to DIEGO'S house.*)

CRISTINA: Diego, I can't do it.

DIEGO: What can't my baby Cristina do?

FRIDA: Must we? (*To DIEGO, commenting on the scene with CRISTINA.*)

DIEGO: (*to FRIDA*) You do it to me, I do it to you.

CRISTINA: (*referring to DIEGO'S gun*) What are you doing?

DIEGO: Going painting.

CRISTINA: I can't do this.

DIEGO: Look, just put income under income and expenditure under expenditure. I'll get Frida to add them up. (*CRISTINA is fed up.*) What? What is it?

CRISTINA: I'm not always sure which is which. Frida was the only one who had an education!

(*A hail of automatic gunfire sends them to the ground. CATARINA parodies the Nazis.*)

VOICES: Long live the Third Reich, Heil Hitler!

CRISTINA: The bastard sons of whores. Give me your gun. (*CRISTINA rushes off firing.*) Oh.... I got one.

SCENE THIRTY-THREE

(*Lights change to Park. FRIDA laughs at DIEGO sprawled on his stomach. He relaxes as if from a nightmare.*)

FRIDA: You do it to me but you always end up flat on your face!

DIEGO: (*to audience*) Don't marry a Kahlo girl, they said. They are all crazy. It was you they wanted to kill, my Frida. They knew better than I what would destroy me.

FRIDA: (*to audience*) Life grew very complex. We had Nazis from the German Embassy shooting at us, Stalinists and, of course, our own government troops were not beyond it.

DIEGO: Some Mexicans we had met in Detroit who, with our help, returned home and set up farms near Acapulco, caught the Nazis. The Nazis were no more.

FRIDA: If you try to kill Diego, don't forget we have many friends, many, many friends.

DIEGO: Friends? You were my only friend, the rest have only ever been allies. That way when they betray me they do not destroy my heart. You alone have that privilege.

FRIDA: Oh, you great martyr. When have I ever betrayed you?

DIEGO: That summer in Paztcuaro when Andre and Jacqueline Breton came from France.

FRIDA: I was bored; all those dreary organised debates with Trotsky in the farmhouse, chief cockerel.

SCENE THIRTY-FOUR

(*FRIDA stirs a large pot of food. DIEGO comes up behind her. She smells him.*)

FRIDA: Go and bathe. Jacqueline and I have cooked a

218

wonderful meal, half french, half Mexican, with a twist of boiled cabbage for old man Trotsky. I thought it might help maintain the wind in his guts.

DIEGO: He is the only man I have ever met with as much energy as me. Breton is exhausted. Have you decided? Frida, you must accept Breton's offer. An exhibition in Paris? You must. I've talked myself dry persuading him.

FRIDA: You just want me out of the way. (*pause*) Sorry.

DIEGO: Forgiven. I need a drink.

FRIDA: After the bath. (*She speaks in a childish voice to him.*) Be a good boy. I bought you something to go in your bath. Something for good boys.

DIEGO: What is is?

FRIDA: Undress first, only good boys get presents.

DIEGO: No. Show me.

FRIDA: Promise to bath, promise?

DIEGO: Promise.

(*She mimes a toy duck. Diego is delighted and makes a quacking sound.*)

FRIDA: Now bath.

DIEGO: No.

FRIDA: What did you say? What did you say? If you get into that bath I will do something very rude to you. I do very rude things to little boys if they are good. Go. I will come and see you in a moment. Now go.

(DIEGO exits. *FRIDA returns to the food. JAC-QUELINE BRETON enters and kisses FRIDA. They are lovers.*)

JACQUELINE: Andre is in a mood.

219

(*FRIDA laughs and gives JACQUELINE a taste of the food.*)

FRIDA: In the States I could not cook us an omelette. I hated electric cookers.

JACQUELINE: Will you accept Andre's offer to exhibit in Paris? You could come and stay with us.

FRIDA: Diego says I should never turn down an opportunity. I have been invited to exhibit in New York as well. Look at me, the big artist!

JACQUELINE: Will you come and stay with us?

(*FRIDA nods and kisses her. NATALIA TROTSKY enters. She is trapped between disturbing their kiss and the impending arrival of the men.*)

NATALIA: Do I smell cabbage? It will be all he eats, I warn you. They are coming in now. He hates anything hot or spicy.

JACQUELINE: Have you a cigarette?

(*FRIDA and JACQUELINE light up cigarettes. FRIDA touches JACQUELINE as if to comfort her. LEON and ANDRE enter. They both love FRIDA. ANDRE suspects that JACQUELINE, his wife, is also his rival for FRIDA. There is tension between them.*)

ANDRE: Frida, why did you leave the discussion? We needed you there. It became loathsome and egotistical. I felt deserted.

LEON: Women shouldn't smoke.

JACQUELINE: (*to TROTSKY*) You are so sweet.

ANDRE: That smells wonderful.

(*FRIDA gives him a taste.*)

NATALIA: I warned them you would not eat anything spicy.

LEON: Frida's cooking has captured my taste buds.

(She gives him a taste.)

ANDRE: Tell him Frida, explain to him, the artist employs intuition and the subconscious mind when creating Art. Consciously or unconsciously they do that. Frida's painting is precisely that, the relationship between inner and outer self, between skin and mind. That is why politicians should stay out of Art. Art is essentially the activity of individuals. It is not the State's business.

TROTSKY: Frida, I hope you do not think me such an ignorant man as to not agree with Andre. But Andre, Frida's images are a response to real situations, not to dreams. She is not a surrealist but a realist.

NATALIA: What do you think, Frida?

JACQUELINE:I think you should both shut up.

FRIDA: In my country people still make things for themselves. In the States, hardly ever, just bits of things. They never see themselves in the objects around them. I hope development does not kill our souls as it has in Detroit. I paint so that I think about who I am and what it feels like to be alive. That is all, nothing special.

ANDRE: I agree with you, Frida.

TROTSKY: So do I, so do I.

JACQUELINE: I thought they might.

NATALIA: Shall we take a walk before dinner?

FRIDA: Yes, please. All of you go.

            (None of the others want to go.)

TROTSKY: Perhaps if you had been there, we would not have become so stubborn.

ANDRE: You would have enjoyed it. Diego sat talking the

221

whole time with a parrot on his head.

FRIDA: I think that parrot was having a joke on you, no?

ANDRE: Very probably. Mexico is the surrealist place par excellence and you, Frida, are its greatest painter, a ribbon around a bomb.

JACQUELINE: Andre, you are drooling.

ANDRE: Drooling, what a perfect word it is when applied correctly.

JACQUELINE: You go. I will stay and help Frida.

ANDRE: Oh, well in that case I will stay as well.

FRIDA: (*to JACQUELINE*) Go, it is all under control now.

(*JACQUELINE goes, unhappily.*)

ANDRE: Are you joining us?

NATALIA: Yes, come Lev Davidovitch, stretch your old legs.

TROTSKY: Start walking, I will be there.

(*She exits begrudgingly on ANDRE'S arm.*)

TROTSKY: Well, have you considered my letter?

FRIDA: Yes, I have.

TROTSKY: What do you think of my proposals? (*She laughs.*) Please. (*He holds her.*) I have spent my whole life as a soldier. You have made me realise that I have missed so much. I have missed you. I cannot work.

FRIDA: Wait, wait, this is very dangerous for you. A scandal would ruin you. Beside, Diego would be consumed by anger and jealousy. He thinks of you as his friend, in his debt.

TROTSKY: We can be careful.

FRIDA: Very, very careful. Well, kiss me then.

(*They kiss. FRIDA screams.*)

TROTSKY: What is it? Did I hurt you?

DIEGO: Frida? (*offstage*)

FRIDA: I burnt my arse on the oven.

DIEGO: Frida?

FRIDA: Out, out!

            (*TROTSKY exits. DIEGO enters.*)

DIEGO: You screamed.

FRIDA: I burnt my arse on the oven.

DIEGO: Come here, I will kiss it better.

FRIDA: You wash your neck, I'll be there to check in a moment. Go, go. I love you.

SCENE THIRTY-FIVE

(*CATARINA takes FRIDA'S hand and introduces an ominous tone before the stage bursts into activity with the entrance of SIQUEIROS and his comrades who, full of high spirits, have arrived in SPAIN. The men sing a "call and response" Mexican style song.*)

SIQUEIROS: A Viva Los Calaveras
           A ribe ribe Los Catalan.

CHORUS: A Viva Los Calaveras
           A ribe ribe Los Catalan.

SIQUEIROS: Socialista Mexicanos come to fight in foreign lands. We're telling all you fascists that today will
                                        be your last.
           We're telling all you fascists that we're gonna kick
           (x2)   your ass.

CHORUS: Today, today, today will be your last

Communista Mexicanos gonna kick your ass.
Siqueiros, don't scare us, we're gonna kick their
ass.
We're telling all the fascists that today will be
their last.

SIQUEIROS: Hey, me amigos, you want to hear my plan?
We're gonna hand the land back to every working
man.
Come you women, it's a time you had a laugh
Soon every fascist will be buried in the past.

CHORUS: At last! At last, all buried in the past.
We're gonna build a peace and you know it's
gonna last.
Siqueiros, don't scare us, we're gonna kick their
ass.
We're telling all the fascists that today will be
their last.
Today, today, today will be your last
Communista Mexicanos gonna kick your ass.
Siqueiros, don't scare us, we're gonna kick their
ass.
We're telling all you fascists that today will be
your last!

(*The mood changes rapidly as the reality of war sends
them, contorting, into a depiction of DIEGO'S 'The
Trench'. FRIDA paints a depiction of her work 'They
Asked For Aeroplanes But Only Got Straw Wings.'
DIEGO reads a letter from SIQUEIROS. They say the
first line together, then SIQUEIROS continues.*)

DIEGO: In Spain Hope stood in rotting boots.

SIQUEIROS: Along the trenches and gutters.
Ran the rumour of disaster
Move along, move along, they are filling with our
corpses.
Poet lays upon worker.
Peasant upon stranger.
The infantry of our hope scythed by artillery.

In Spain.
Hope stood in rotting boots
And looked up
Reaching for the sun with fists
To pluck out aeroplanes sent by Hitler!
Mexican and Spaniard
Australian and Frenchman
Welsh miner and German Jew
Lay arms entwined,
In death an image for the living
To ponder and ask the question
What now?

SCENE THRITY-SIX

(*Lights return to the Park.*)

FRIDA: They asked for aeroplanes but only got straw wings.

DIEGO: After Spain we knew we were heading for a World War.

FRIDA: Everywhere division. Divorce was part of it. You and your movie stars. (*to Audience*) I'm surprised he wasn't in *Baedeker's Guide to Mexico*. No gringo debutante tourist had done Mexico until they had seen the Zocolo, had a tequilla and fucked old Diego Rivera.

DIEGO: Well, who was the one to screw old man Trotsky? You didn't give a damn about his wife, did you?

SCENE THIRTY-SEVEN

(*Lights up on NATALIA and LEON.*)

NATALIA: I cannot imagine it. You and her, I can't imagine you. All the places on my body that are for you, I cannot imagine you being.... perhaps I can imagine it. I can see you touching her. You have betrayed me so badly, Lev Davidovitch. I watched them murder my children one by one because of who you were. Our babies! You owed me something, didn't you? You are all I have left of my life's work. Now that has been trespassed, given away.

LEON: Nata....

NATALIA: No. Don't you at least owe me integrity? You owe me my dignity. I am not colourful and flamboyant. I am not Bohemian, but I have warmed away your troubles and loved you since I was a girl. But there is nothing, no part of you which is mine... except perhaps that part of you which is pure scum, perhaps you have saved me that much. I want to know what you plan.

SCENE THIRTY-EIGHT

(*The Park.*)

DIEGO: (*to audience*) It soon became apparent that the political differences between Trotsky and myself were irreconcilable. (*to FRIDA*) I want a divorce!

FRIDA: No!

DIEGO: I am in love with Paulette Goddard. She plans to leave Charlie Chaplin for me!

FRIDA AND DIEGO

FRIDA: Have her! Have her! I am going to Paris. I don't need you anymore! I am in love with a Spanish refugee! He wants me to have his children!

(They go to their separate sides of the stage.)

DIEGO: I have always kept love outside the house
Outside, in the yard
But could never close the door.
Love, confused
Would enter and lay by the fire.
Much to my relief.
But when I was tired of love
I could turn around and say
What are you doing in the house?
You know you've no right to be in here!
Get out you stupid creature!
Love would bolt, whimpering.
And I would wait by the fire
Hoping love would dare to enter again.

FRIDA: I have always been doubly punished for loving you.

SCENE THIRTY-NINE

(Two CALAVERAS become the painting of the 'Two Frida's'. One is suggestive of Europe, the other, of Mexico's Indians. FRIDA creates the image with red ribbon to indicate blood lines.)

FRIDA: I am the two Fridas.

FRIDA 1: *(European)* I am my father from across the seas.

FRIDA 2: My mother and her Indian land.

ALL: I am Mexico
First and foremost I am Mexico,

227

I am a Mexican woman.
This is what my life is like
My name is Frida Kahlo. .

(*FRIDA joins the hands of the FRIDAS 1 and 2 as they form a depiction. They do not acknowledge DIEGO, who looks on.*)

DIEGO: Frida? Frida? You have conquered the Louvre. Picasso wrote to me, Kandinsky wept at your exhibition, so I hear. You have worked hard, you deserve it. Picasso said, "Neither you Diego, nor I, could paint a head like Frida Kahlo can."

(*A long silence. CATARINA is confused. She signals the CALAVERAS to bring on DR ELOESSER. They deposit him with his boat, confused, mid stage.*)

SCENE FORTY

ELOESSER: Excuse me, Diego.

DIEGO: Dr Eloesser.

ELOESSER: Frida is very ill. She needs treatment to prevent gangrene in her right foot. In Mexico she has operations she doesn't need! Why? Ask yourself, why? To show you her pain. (*to FRIDA*) Frida, look at him, all the women of San Francisco clammering to meet him but is he happy? He is painting all the hours he can to overcome his misery. If you want him you have to love him for what he is, not for what he isn't, and Diego is not, nor ever will be anybody's husband; loyalty, fidelity, monogamy, forget it.

DIEGO: Come to San Francisco. This divorce is a disaster. Marry me again.

FRIDA: There are conditions.
I pay half the household expenses.
I support myself financially.
That we never have sex.
I want something of you that no-one else has.

DIEGO: I need you to have that.

(*CATARINA and the CALAVERAS encourage FRIDA and DIEGO to kiss. When they do so, they erupt into a joyful dance.*)

SCENE FORTY-ONE

(*SIQUEIROS enters with a gun and takes the hands of CATARINA. He sings.*)

SIQUEIROS: La Calavera, Calavera!

Oh La Pelona
I've always known ya would do what was wanted.
Would dance on the grave of the one who is hunted.
Siqueiros got a gun
Siqueiros got a gun
Oh La Pelona!
If I could phone ya, I'd rattle your bones with
news of a murder
A traitor's escaped, he slides like a snake but now
gets no further
Siqueiros got a gun
Siqueiros got a gun

(*The song ends.*)

Hey, Trotsky, the boys are back from Spain!

(*He fires into the audience.*)

229

SCENE FORTY-TWO

(*Lights up on the Park.*)

DIEGO: And from the rumbling clouds
Came news
Hitler was at war.
Time to take stock
To invest in the future.

(*CATARINA leads FRIDA towards her bed. FRIDA sickens and gets into her bed. The CALAVERAS become her students, LOS FRIDOS.*)

FRIDA: I don't know how to teach you. All I want you to do is look very carefully and gain a feeling about the thing you are looking at. Create a mood for yourself before you ever put a mark on paper. An artist never draws an object, they draw their feelings for it. In this way we make a strong relationship with the world. A strong life force. We feed. Unless we feed, we shrivel up and die, whole societies can die. We are Mexican artists, look at Mexico.

DIEGO: In those years you poured your life into images. Did you know your day was coming to a close? Did you know? It was that operation, that was it, that's what did it.

(*The CALAVERAS now lurk about her bed. Their movements suggest a dream-like drug-induced state. CRISTINA enters.*)

FRIDA: Cristina! Cristina, hold my hand when they anaesthetise me, hold my hand. I am sinking, sinking under the weight of those who look at me. Bring the children to see me when I wake up. Tree of hope stay firm. Don't let them bury me lying down, I cannot bear the thought of eternity in this position. Burn me, burn me to ashes.

CRISTINA: Frida? Frida? Can you hear me?

DOCTOR: Keep her dose of Morphine on the decline. We didn't operate to send her out a drug addict.

(*FRIDA screams with pain.*)

CRISTINA: Help her! Help her! She is in pain!

(*FRIDA appears to come round. A young FRIDA appears with straw wings. She is trying to fly. Her movements are slow. Her MOTHER and FATHER appear. The CALAVERAS draw red ribbons forth from their hands and link them to FRIDA.*)

FRIDA: Let me lie by the doors so that I can see my
                                                       garden.
There I played as a girl
Learnt to walk.
There is my mother, forever condemning me.
There is my father, lost in his own mind.
(*She drifts back into a haze.*)
Trotsky murdered in Coyoacán?
(*A silhouette of Trotsky being murdered.*)
Who's Diego with? Dolores Del Rio? Maria Felix?

(*The haze clears for a moment as DIEGO speaks.*)

DIEGO: Seriously, I have never known anything like it. There I was, painting 'Dream of a Sunday Afternoon in The Alameda Park' and she walks in. A total stranger and claims her child is mine. I looked at it and could not see the slightest resemblance.

FRIDA: What did you do?

DIEGO: I painted the child on the mural, holding her doll. That seemed to satisfy everyone.

(*They laugh. FRIDA drifts into a haze.*)

LUPE: Frida? Frida? It's me, Lupe.

FRIDA: Tell your brother, el doctor, I won't be needing

231

	any more abortions. I have dried up. It is over.
LUPE:	It's not such a bad thing.
FRIDA:	Not so bad? To know it's over, that I never did it. Lost my chance. I want to go back. I want to go back. Please, let me try one more time.
LUPE:	Stop it, Frida, can you hear me?
FRIDA:	I've counted. Twenty pregnancies, see I could have had one if I'd wanted, easy. I feel dry inside. Give me Demerol.
LUPE:	Where is it?
FRIDA:	In that drawer. There, yes, open it. No, that's it, now take a syringe as well, that's it.
LUPE:	I can't do this.
FRIDA:	It's all right, I'll show you how.
LUPE:	But I hate anything to do with injections.
FRIDA:	Look, you stupid cow, I need it!
DIEGO:	Frida, why? You are killing yourself. Frida!
DOCTOR:	We have waited as long as we could.
	(*DIEGO cries.*)
FRIDA:	Diego? What? What is it?
DOCTOR:	The gangrene. We have no option but to amputate your right leg.
FRIDA:	No! (*She screams.*)
DIEGO:	This will kill her. My little bird, what have they done to you?
FRIDA:	Give me a cigarette. Cut it off, I have wings, they cannot stop me flying. Cut it off. Cristina, don't let go of my hand.
DIEGO:	Friducita. Guess what? There is to be huge fiesta. Frida Kahlo is to have her first retrospective

232

exhibition in her own country. There will be thousands there to see you.

FRIDA: You want me to stay alive for that?

CRISTINA: Frida, are you ready?

FRIDA: Carry me there in my bed! Christina! Hold my hand.

(*CRISTINA does so. The CALAVERAS move as if in a drug-induced haze once again.*)

FRIDA: The anaesthetic is working
I am falling, falling.
The lights are fading.
Hold me up, hold me up, I want to paint.
I must paint.

(*FRIDA sees CALAVERA CATARINA who leads the haunting.*)

I will fight
I will fight
La Pelona.
The aunt of the little girls, blows kisses that
                            tingle my skin.
But she has not caught me yet.
Viva la Vida,
Viva la Vida!
It hurts!
Diego!
Diego has started a protest,
We will stop this bomb.
Thank God I knew Diego.
My camarade.
Diego, beginning
Diego, constructor
Diego, my baby
Diego, my boyfriend
Diego, painter
My lover

My husband
Friend
Diego, my mother
Diego, on my mind
Where is he?
Always leaving, always.

Demerol, give me Demerol. It doesn't matter now.
Just so that I can see my exhibition, please? It was
my leg they put in the incinerator. I have a right!

SCENE FORTY-THREE

(*The Exhibition. The CALAVERAS applaud.*)

CRISTINA: Frida, everyone wants to congratulate you. Hundreds of people are here, the street is crowded. Your exhibition, I had no idea.

DIEGO: To see it all in one place, even I am astonished.

FRIDA: I am the wounded deer
Who lives on the mountain
The little deer gazing at a rocky pool
At what the water gave me.
The wounded deer
Who comes down the mountain slope each night
And into your hut
To lay beside you till the morning.

DOCTOR: We should really take you home, Senora Kahlo.

DIEGO: Touch her and I'll kill you.

(*THE CALAVERAS hiss and retract. FRIDA and DIEGO are alone by the bed.*)

FRIDA: Was my exhibition a great success?

DIEGO: A very great success. Frida, you are a better painter than I. For the first time in Art we have

234

the biology of a woman's experience. Beauty and savagery.

FRIDA: Here, I want you to have this now. For our twenty-fifth wedding anniversay.

           (*She gives him a ring.*)

DIEGO: But we have ten days yet.

FRIDA: Have it now. I love you more than myself. I wish it could be for longer.

DIEGO: I know, I know.

           (*They kiss. This is goodbye and DIEGO realises it. As they kiss the CALAVERAS, led by CATARINA, whisper urgently.*)

CALAVERA:Look mummy, that tram.

CALAVERA:Hey, look out!!

CALAVERA:What's the driver doing? Hey? Mind out! That tram!

CALAVERA:Stop!

           (*FRIDA is dead. DIEGO slowly rises and turns towards the audience. We are back at the beginning of the play. Lights fade until, once again DIEGO stands in a single light.*)

DIEGO: Here we stand before you to take the bow
           But which way now?
           My father bought a silver mine
           One day the mine ran out of silver
           Which way now?
           In the air of Mexico City hangs poison
           And in the arsenals of generals
           The last seed to be opened on the earth.
           Whilst in the Park the beggars still hold out their
                                                      hands.
           Which way now?
           For in my eyes last night we lost Cauhtemoc's life

In my eyes last night Cauhtemoc died
And today?
Today we need to dream a little in the
                              Alameda Park.

(*DIEGO hands the paint brush towards the audience,
offering it to them. He is acknowledging the end of his
era. He is handing over the tools of creativity hoping
someone will carry on the struggle. The lights fade to
black. The CALAVERAS form the mural 'Dream of a
Sunday Afternoon in The Alameda Park'. Lights up.
DIEGO takes his place beside FRIDA. The cast reprise
the Barrel Organ waltz.*)

(*THE END.*)

Acknowledgements

The author wishes to thank the many Mid Powys Youth Theatre members who brought these plays to life, Theatr Powys and the Wyeside Arts Centre for providing space and resources, The Arts Council of Wales and Powys County Council and to my professional collaborators who made the plays work.

A particular thanks to John Egglestone and Lynn Farr, teachers who released my potential and saved my life.

These plays are dedicated to Lesley Smith, Johanna Quinn, Allie Saunders, Patricia and Thomas Cullen whose love is present in every moment, even now.

About the Author

Greg Cullen was born into the Irish community in London. He was educated at Blessed John Southworth and Heathcote Secondary School in Stevenage. Later he attended St. Mary's University College, Strawberry Hill, studying Drama, Art and Education.

In 1983 he became writer-in-residence with Theatr Powys for whom he wrote a wide variety of plays including 'Taken Out'. In 1987 he founded Mid Powys Youth Theatre for whom he has also written the award-winning 'Raging Angels', 'Little Devils' and 'Whispers in the Woods'.

In 1992 he was appointed writer-in-residence at the Welsh College of Music and Drama for whom he wrote 'An Informer's Duty'.

Adaptations include 'Silas Marner', 'Hard Times', 'A Christmas Carol', 'Germinal' and 'Under Goliath'.

Radio Plays include 'Tower', 'The Whistleblower', 'New World in the Mourning', 'Spoiled Papers' and 'Taken Out'.

In 1997, 'Birdbrain', a short film, won the BBC/Wales Film Council 'PICS' competition and a BAFTA award. He is currently writing a full length film.

Greg Cullen has one son and lives in mid Wales.